A SUBTLE MURDER

BLYTHE BAKER

M rs. Worthing threw her head back in laughter, nearly losing her close-fitted hat. The sound echoed off the pristine white floors and ceilings, and I resisted the urge to press my hands into my ears to block the noise. Somewhere near nineteen million people lived in Bombay, and nearly every single one of them seemed to be milling around in the embassy lobby. Government workers in black suits and long coats, despite the heat, rushed by, anxious to get where they were going. As was I.

I'd been waiting in the lobby for half an hour and, while Mrs. Worthing beside me seemed to be enjoying chatting with nearby strangers, the exposure of the open space made my skin itch. All I wanted was to put a safe cushion of several thousand miles between myself and India.

I scanned the passing crowd as closely as I was willing, keeping an eye out for a familiar white boater hat with a red grosgrain ribbon. The crowd in the lobby parted for a moment, just long enough for me to catch my own reflection in a mirror on the opposite wall. I looked as I always had, curly blond hair cropped around my heart-shaped face, lips dark burgundy and plump. Except for the jagged scar running across my cheek, the bone slightly dented in from being fractured. That was new.

Suddenly, the embassy fell away, drifting out of sight like a fog, replaced by the crowded streets of Simla, the summer capital of British India. I sat in the backseat of a tightly packed car, pressed against the door. My shoulder ached from the squeeze, but a breeze rolled through the window and cooled my flushed skin. Soldiers and civil servants of the British Raj, along with their wives and families, often passed the hot season in the cool foothills of the Himalayas, but the day still felt balmy and I was grateful for the air rushing through the window.

Everyone in the car was laughing and talking, filling the small space with their warm breath, but I ignored them, favoring the scenes outside the window. Colorful buildings lined the wide dirt road, blurring together in a rainbow as we drove. But then, suddenly, the car lurched to a stop. A mass of people had formed in the street and traffic had come to a standstill. I couldn't wait until we began moving again so I could feel the air pour through the window once more.

Slowly, the crowd began to disperse, and our car cut a slow, torturous path through them. People were pressed right up against the sides of the vehicle, and I worried we would run over their vibrantly colored summer linens.

Then, a man separated himself from the crowd. He was an Indian draped in plain-colored rags that hung from him in limp tatters. A beggar. I was examining his clothes so intently that I didn't realize he was staring at me until he began moving towards our car, his bare feet kicking up tiny clouds of dust with every step. The conversation in the car continued as the man lifted his arms above his head, something pressed delicately between his fingers, and tossed an object through the open window of our vehicle.

I said nothing for a few seconds as my mind attempted to find a rationale for the man's actions. However, there was none. I turned to the rest of the passengers in the car, watched as their carefree smiles melted into confusion, everyone turning towards the small object that had landed in the far corner of the front seat. A woman in the back beside me, a beautiful blond girl, opened her mouth in a scream, but the explosion drowned out the sound.

Ringing filled my ears and a sharp pain slashed across my cheek. My body curled in on itself as everything descended into chaos. After a few moments, I opened my eyes to see nothing but a brown haze of smoke and dust. I looked back towards where the girl next to me had just been, but I could no longer see her face. The seat beside me was now empty. Except it wasn't. The smoke cleared for only a second before reconstituting, but it was long enough for me to see a blood-spattered hand lying on the seat next to me. A scream burned in the back of my throat.

"Are my little travelers ready?"

The voice jerked me back to the present. I was sitting on a low wooden bench along a wall of the embassy in Bombay, the busy streets of Simla having been only in my memory. Mr. Worthing was standing in front of me. He wore a white linen suit and a white boater hat, the red grosgrain ribbon matching his bowtie, which squeezed his neck and gave him the appearance of an overstuffed sausage. Mr. Worthing had worked at the embassy until the last hour, during which time he had tendered his resignation.

"Did everything go smoothly, dear?" Mrs. Worthing asked, waving goodbye to the near-strangers she'd made acquaintance with while waiting for Mr. Worthing to arrive.

"Absolutely," Mr. Worthing said. "All arrangements have been made for our departure. England awaits."

"Then let us not waste another minute," Mrs. Worthing said. "Walk with me, Rose." She looped her arm through mine, and together we walked out the embassy doors and loaded into a waiting car that was filled to the brim with our luggage.

~

THE *RMS STAR of India* was visible long before we reached the docks. Mr. Worthing talked incessantly about the ship as we neared it.

"A luxury liner, finest ship to ever set sail from India. Carries everything from passengers to cargo and royal mail," he said. And then, at Mrs. Worthing's displeasure at the thought of being stuffed into a room like a piece of mail, Mr. Worthing added, "Do not fret, my dear. All of that is below deck. We are in first class."

Mr. and Mrs. Worthing were an odd couple—where Mrs. Worthing was all gossip and status, Mr. Worthing was a man of facts. They rarely agreed on anything, but they loved each other deeply, and I was grateful for their company. They had volunteered to act as my chaperones for the three-week duration of the voyage, ensuring I made it safely to London.

I began to see more and more people along the sides of the road carrying steamer trunks and luggage, headed for the ship. I could count each of the six decks of the ship towering over us as the driver pulled the car over on the side of the road not far from the docks. The hull of the vessel was black, like a giant's freshly shined shoe, and looked to be over 500-feet long with black and red funnels stretching from the top of the ship into the sky. I'd never seen a vessel so big.

"Out you come, Rose," Mr. Worthing said. I turned and realized he and Mrs. Worthing had already exited the vehicle, and his hand was outstretched toward me. I took it and stepped into the road. "Wonderful, isn't it?"

"Absolutely," I answered, smiling up at him.

"The ship boasts six-hundred passengers, not including crew, and has all the modern amenities. The vessel's quadruple-expansion engines guarantee a speedy voyage, as we pass through the Suez Canal, stopping at the ports of Aden, Said, Malta, Marseilles, and Gibraltar along the way," he continued, sounding like a tour guide.

"Stop boring the girl," Mrs. Worthing said. "If she's anything like me, she only cares about the Turkish bath and the indoor swimming pool."

We unloaded our luggage and Mr. Worthing tried to impress upon his wife the magnificence of the ship we were about to board, but it was obvious she cared little about what he was saying.

Mr. Worthing insisted he carry our luggage, so Mrs. Worthing and I walked slowly behind him as he struggled under the weight of our things. As we neared the gangplank, a young crewman, long and tan and blond, walked down towards us and offered assistance.

"Oh, sure," Mr. Worthing said, shrugging as though it didn't matter to him whether he received a drop of help or not, though sweat had begun to bead on his forehead, dripping from under his hat. "Might as well."

"Tip the man," Mrs. Worthing said, nudging her husband between the ribs with her pointy elbow.

The door at the top of the gangplank stood open for now, but soon it would close and I would be on my way to

England. I'd come to India as a child and I was sad to say goodbye. However, recent events had made me eager for a fresh start. While Mr. and Mrs. Worthing dug through pockets and luggage, looking for a suitable tip for the young crewman, I turned and looked down at the country I was leaving behind, knowing it would likely be for the very last time.

During my reverie, a woman still on the ground, but heading for the ship, caught my attention. Her dark hair, covered with a white cloche hat, was tucked into a bun at the base of her neck, and she wore a light blue tea gown with loose sleeves that cuffed at her wrists. The woman was giddy, practically skipping towards the ship, smiling and waving to everyone as she passed. I wanted to turn away and roll my eyes at her lack of decorum, but something about her eyes stopped me. She cast sidelong glances at the crowd, as if she were expecting someone to jump out at her. Her smile faltered ever so slightly as she caught sight of someone in the crowd, but quickly she whipped her head back around and grinned.

"Miss?"

The blond crewmember was smiling at me, beckoning me into the ship where Mr. and Mrs. Worthing were waiting for me.

I turned back to find the woman again, but she had disappeared into the line of passengers waiting to board. Something about her had set me on edge, but that didn't take much these days. I touched my ruined cheekbone with the tip of my gloved finger for just a second, and then pushed the woman from my mind.

I accepted the hand of the crewmember and stepped over the threshold and into the *RMS Star of India*. In three weeks time, I would be in London with my inheritance and an entirely new life. No need to dwell on the old one.

I WANTED to explore the ship, but Mrs. Worthing insisted we go immediately to our stateroom and freshen up. Our tickets were in first class, so our room looked more like a flat than the boarding room I'd been imagining. I had my own private washroom and sleeping cabin with a door that lead to a shared sitting room where Mrs. Worthing and I agreed to meet in fifteen minutes.

I unpacked my steamer trunk into mahogany drawers built into the wall, and arranged my dresses on hangers in a modest but suitable closet. The cabin was small, but I couldn't imagine I'd be spending much time in there with an entire ship to explore.

The yellow washroom light left much to be desired, but it would have to do for the next few weeks. I rarely used mirrors, anyway. At least, not until recently. Since the explosion, I checked my reflection several times a day to be sure the cream and powder was still in place over the scar on my cheek. I would never be able to completely hide the damage that had been done, but makeup did help disguise it, at least from a distance.

I ran my finger over the uneven skin, remembering the blood that had poured down my face and neck, the raw flesh that had been stitched together in the hospital while I faded in and out of consciousness. It was a miracle I'd survived at all. The bomb had been only a few feet away, having landed near the lap of—

A scream. For a moment I thought I'd imagined the sound, that perhaps the trauma had worked itself into my mind and twisted it, confusing past and present. Was I going mad, my nerves finally consuming me after weeks of flashbacks and nightmares?

Then, I heard a man's voice. I pressed my hand to my heart, trying to slow its thunderous beat. The sound was coming from the state room next to mine. A man and woman were in the midst of a violent argument. I pressed my ear to the wall, but I couldn't make out the words. Suddenly, the ship's horn blew, sending me flying away from the wall. I laughed at my own skittishness, and then glanced once more in the mirror before hurrying to the sitting room to meet Mrs. Worthing.

We rushed up to the deck to watch as the ship pulled away from the dock. Fellow passengers pressed against the black railings and waved down to the crowd still onshore. Mrs. Worthing left after only a minute or two, while we were still close enough to land to see each individual face looking up at the ship. I, however, stayed behind. I wanted to watch India fade into the horizon, become a green blur in the distance. The sea wind swept across the deck and made me shiver, but still I stayed at the railing. When most everyone had cleared off to explore the ship and settle in, I lingered, lifting one hand and waving at the country I'd called home for so long. Saying goodbye to the trauma of my past.

When I finally turned, I felt lighter, though my ordeal was nowhere near over. India was in my past, but England lay ahead. I could only hope I had the courage to face the challenges that awaited.

2

I spent the afternoon marveling at the size and grandeur of the *RMS Star of India*. The Promenade deck, reserved exclusively for first class passengers, provided endless opportunity for the wealthy to lounge and consume, whether it be snacks, cigarettes, or tea. Wooden double doors lead from the outer deck to a wood-paneled salon where businessmen and present and past government officials sat in a loose circle discussing the British Raj and the post-war economy. I decided not to linger after one of the men, a walrus-like man with a thick beard, glared at me as though I'd interrupted their discussion by releasing an especially malodorous smell.

Wind blew across the ship, whipping skirts and making men hold onto their hats, but it was a refreshing change from the Indian summer. Many passengers were making use of the veranda café, sipping tea and starters while enjoying the cool sea air. Wooden beams stretched from the center of the ship out towards the railing, and a red and white striped fabric draped across them, providing shade. This was where Mrs. Worthing had decided to pass the time until dinner. As

I walked by—quickly, so as not to be pulled into her conversation—she had already made several new friends and was
laughing riotously, drawing the ire of every nearby
passenger who wasn't part of the group.

The rest of the A Deck was devoted to a smoking room,
complete with a fireplace and exorbitant Persian rugs, and a
reading and music room where I saw one man trying and
failing to read while a woman attempted to play the piano
on the opposite end of the room. The ship boasted many
other amenities, too many to even think about all at once,
but I made my way to the bow of the craft where I found a
wicker lounge chair to occupy until dinner. Three weeks at
sea meant I would have more than enough time to discover
every nook and cranny of the ship, and all of the driving and
unpacking had left me feeling drained. I lay back in the
chair, crossed my ankles, closed my eyes, and let the afternoon sun warm my skin.

A LOUD HORN SOUNDED, startling me from my accidental
nap. I opened my eyes and noticed everyone rising from
their seats and stretching. While I'd been asleep, many of
the women had changed from afternoon tea dresses into
floor length evening gowns, and the men wore dark suits
and hats.

"Jane, honestly. Go and change for dinner before we
are late."

I turned to see an elderly woman in a green velvet gown
leading a young girl of about sixteen by the neck. The shape
and material of the gown hugged the woman's bumpy mid-
section in a rather unflattering way and her voice was shrill
and harsh like steam escaping a kettle as she prodded the

young girl along. As I watched them, the woman cast her hawk-like, watery eyes at me, giving me a good look from top to bottom.

"You ought to go change, as well," she said, giving me her unsolicited opinion. "The dinner bell just rang. That is the sound that disturbed your nap, if you weren't already aware."

The woman didn't speak as harshly to me as she did to the young girl, but she made it clear my presence on the ship brought her little joy.

I smiled at her, a fake toothy grin. "Thank you, ma'am. I did hear the bell, but I follow the fashionable custom of never arriving anywhere perfectly on time."

That earned me a scowl from the woman and a curious glance from the young girl. I smiled at her, but the older woman almost immediately had her hand back on the girl's neck, directing her away from me as though I had the plague and another second in my company would be the end of both of them.

Back in my cabin, I changed into a floor-length burgundy satin gown with ruched gold lamé layered on top. Fine gold embroidery decorated the handkerchief hem and the deep-cut neckline. I paired it with a delicate lace headband that helped to keep my curls tame. The humidity out at sea had given them more volume than normal. Finally, I checked my makeup once more in the mirror, and then slipped into a pair of gold t-strap shoes before darting out of the stateroom and up to the deck. I wasn't the last passenger into the dining room, but the deck crowd had considerably thinned, and it took a few minutes of searching to find Mr. and Mrs. Worthing sitting at a table in the center of the room, their necks craned in search of me.

As soon as I spotted Mr. and Mrs. Worthing, my fear of

being late and making a fool of myself in front of the other passengers began to wane, and I was able to look around and appreciate my surroundings. The dining room sat at the heart of the ship. The ceiling stretched up two-decks, making the room feel impossibly large, and stained-glass skylights filtered the evening light into watery blues and reds and greens. It felt as though I'd stepped into a Monet painting. A grand walnut staircase was built into the back wall, a centerpiece around which the entire room was arranged. Women moved down the stairs carefully, either escorted by a male counterpart, their arms wrapped together, or with a delicate hand resting on the banister.

"Rose, dear, you ought to take your seat." Mrs. Worthing had appeared at my side without my notice. She looped her arm through mine and we navigated around the tables, tossing polite smiles to everyone we passed. "The program tonight is a buffet. I wish I had known, so I could have saved this dress for a nicer evening."

Mrs. Worthing wore a pale gold velvet number with a drop waist and a white satin rose pinned at her hip. A long string of pearls were strategically wound around her neck several times and bouncing against her chest as we walked. She must have noticed the attention I was paying to them, because she grasped the pearls and whispered, "Imitation. Mr. Worthing has the real things stowed away in the cargo hold. He won't let me wear anything too expensive when we travel. Thieves love to prey on distracted people on holiday."

The table seated eight, and every chair was filled with strangers, except for the ones reserved for Mrs. Worthing and myself. At least, the other diners were strangers to me. Mrs. Worthing, on the other hand, seemed to have formed hasty friendships already, in her usual way.

"Look who I found wandering around the ship," Mrs.

Worthing said, winking at me. She addressed the table. "This is our beloved Rose Beckingham."

I smiled at everyone, though I faltered for a moment when I noticed the harsh elderly woman from the ship deck sitting next to Mr. Worthing. The young girl she'd been with on the deck sat next to her, eyes downcast, looking miserable. She introduced herself as Lady Dixon, and the young girl as her niece, Jane. Next to Jane sat Dr. Rushforth. He was an army surgeon who had a self-important expression, though he didn't look like anyone of any consequence. His nose came to a point far away from the canvas of his face and, paired with his sparse facial hair, gave him the appearance of a weasel.

"You'll have to excuse Colonel Stratton and myself," Dr. Rushforth said, gesturing to the square-shaped man sitting next to him. "We are used to the company of army men. Rarely are we so blessed as to be surrounded by so many charming ladies."

Mrs. Worthing giggled. "Nonsense. Colonel Stratton is fortunate enough to be in the near-constant company of one of the most charming women I've ever met." She smiled at the petite brunette woman sitting next to the colonel, eating noodles with her dessert fork.

The petite woman's mistake in silverware was enough of a distraction that it took me a touch longer than normal to look into her face. When I did, I realized I'd seen her before. Colonel Stratton's wife was the woman I'd seen as I was boarding the ship. I studied her delicate face again, but saw no sign of the fear I'd detected there before.

Lady Dixon scoffed at what she clearly believed to be an unearned compliment, though she disguised it well enough as a cough. On some level, even I had to admit the old woman had a point. Although I'd been with plenty of women less civilized, the Colonel's wife wasn't especially charming when she ate. She struck me as a woman living beyond her class.

The colonel put his thick arm around his wife and stiffly pulled her into his side. "My Ruby is a gem, that's for sure."

The table laughed at his play on words, Mrs. Worthing nearly choking on her sip of wine, but I refrained, instead busying my mouth with my own drink. His joke felt rehearsed, as if he'd said it to a thousand tables before ours. Ruby, I noticed, also didn't laugh. She did, however, do her best to pull her lips into a tight smile in response to the table's admiration of her husband, and then looked past him to steal a glance at Dr. Rushforth. When she noticed he was looking at her—as was the rest of the table—she quickly disentangled herself from her husband and pushed her food around her plate.

Aside from the single joke, the Colonel stayed quiet the rest of the meal, giving his full attention to the food in front of him, standing to return to the buffet whenever his plate was empty. Unlike the rest of the ship's passengers, Colonel Stratton didn't seem to mind the judging stares that followed those who made more than one trip to the buffet. His wife blushed every time he stretched his plump limbs and rose to his feet to get another helping, and I noticed her eyes continued to find Dr. Rushforth, though he had settled into a conversation with Lady Dixon and was not paying her any more attention.

"We all have to survive on the food aboard this ship for the next three weeks," Mr. Worthing whispered to his wife while the Colonel was out of his seat for the third time. "If he doesn't slow down, we'll all starve."

Mrs. Worthing was spared the trouble of reprimanding her husband by the arrival of the ship's captain. He had been greeting passengers and meandering through the dining room since the start of dinner service, but had finally made his way to our table. Captain Croft looked nothing like the ship captain I'd drawn up in my imagination. He didn't have snow white hair or a white beard. He didn't have a thick, indiscernible accent that marked him as a world traveler. Rather, Captain Croft had a strong chin and brow to match, with a well-oiled sweep of black hair, both on top of his head and above his lip. Even when smiling—and his smile was as straight and pearly white as they came—he looked as though he were contemplating something important, his lips pouted and eyes narrowed in a smolder.

"How is the food?" Captain Croft asked, raising an eyebrow at the way Colonel Stratton was shredding his chicken from the bone.

"Marvelous," Mrs. Worthing said. "Finest meal I've had in a good long while."

"Not nearly as fine as your navigating, Captain," Ruby purred, her wide eyes blinking slowly at the handsome man. She seemed to have forgotten all about the presence of her husband. "I'm usually horribly seasick by this point in the trip, but I feel perfectly well."

This marked the first time I'd heard Ruby's voice, which was both high-pitched and nasally, a truly dizzying combination. I recognized it almost immediately as the voice I'd heard coming from the cabin next to me just before the dinner bell.

The Stratton couple made an unusual pair. Ruby, beautiful and expressive, fawned over the Captain while her husband, a scowl etched into the hard stone of his face, shoveled chicken into his mouth. Colonel Stratton hadn't spoken enough for me to be certain he was the man I'd heard Ruby arguing with, but it seemed a likely guess.

My attention was stolen away from Ruby and the Captain by the mention of something I'd hoped to leave in my past.

"So, what really happened in Simla this summer?" Lady Dixon asked Mrs. Worthing. "One hears such dreadful stories of violence."

Mrs. Worthing glanced at me quickly, and blushed when she realized I'd heard. Mr. Worthing, to his credit, attempted to change the subject.

"Violence is everywhere, Lady Dixon. I heard rumor of a violent thief aboard a ship only a few weeks ago," Mr. Worthing said. "I only hope we are among more docile company."

Lady Dixon wouldn't be redirected, though. She remained intent on her subject. "But you and Mrs. Worthing were in Simla during the recent attack, were you not?"

"It was an isolated but unfortunate incident," Mrs. Worthing said. "We don't want to sour the mood of the entire table with such talk."

"Nonsense, I'm asking directly," Lady Dixon said, clearly growing impatient. "Tell me."

"A government minister was murdered by a local extremist," Mr. Worthing said sharply.

"A bomb?" Lady Dixon asked, though it was clear she already knew the answer.

The Worthings nodded slowly, looking down in their laps. We hadn't spent much time discussing the incident, so they had no idea how I would react. Jane, too, seemed uncomfortable, swirling her spoon around the rim of a small cup of soup in front of her, but never eating any.

"Were you with the Worthings in Simla?" Lady Dixon asked.

It took me a few seconds to realize she was talking to me.

"Yes, I was there." Suddenly, my throat felt tight. My heart pressed against my rib cage, threatening to rip through the delicate fabric of my gown.

"Now, perhaps it should be obvious," the old woman said. "But how are you all related?"

Mr. and Mrs. Worthing looked at one another and me, trying to decide how to explain our situation in a manner that wouldn't send me into a fit of tears. I decided to spare them, and perhaps, at the same time, teach Lady Dixon to mind her own business.

"The murdered government minister was my father." I dropped the words on the table like the bomb the revolutionary had lobbed through the car window. "He was killed along with my mother when a bomb exploded. I was the only one in the car who survived."

Lady Dixon's face paled, and she shifted in her seat uncomfortably. For a moment I was pleased to witness her discomfort, but talking about the explosion sobered my mood. I could still hear the ringing in my ears, smell the smoke and charred flesh. I shook my head slightly, a single blonde curl escaping from my headband and brushing against my scarred cheek.

The old woman coughed, but her niece, Jane, sat forward, her cold soup forgotten. "How did you find your way to this ship with the Worthings then?"

Lady Dixon snapped her head towards Jane and leveled a glare at her, but Jane didn't seem to notice. Her eyes were wide and focused on me as though I were the single most interesting person she'd ever met. Unlike with Lady Dixon, Jane's curiosity felt endearing. I couldn't help but answer her.

"I only just survived the explosion, and was left to make a slow recovery in the hospital at Simla. Luckily, the

Worthings were nearby and when they heard of my plight they offered to accompany me to England," I said.

Mrs. Worthing hummed in agreement. "Mr. Worthing recently retired, and we wanted to return to England, anyway. So, it only made sense to see Rose on her journey. We contacted her living relations in London and informed them she would be arriving in three weeks, and booked her a ticket on the *RMS Sar of India*."

"How did you hear of Rose's story?" Jane asked, ignoring the sharp jab in her side from Lady Dixon.

"I worked with Rose's father in government service for years," Mr. Worthing said. "Fine, fine man. It was our honor to assist his only daughter in her greatest time of need. I only wish the good deed hadn't been necessary at all."

"As do we all," Mrs. Worthing said, giving me a sad smile. "Though, I am glad we had the chance to meet and get to know Rose. We knew her mother and father well, but we never had the opportunity to meet Rose until after the tragedy occurred."

"You two are too kind. Truly, these weeks would have been much darker without you both," I said, squeezing Mrs. Worthing's hand under the table. "Please, excuse me for a moment."

I stood on shaky legs and moved across the dining room towards what I hoped to be the ladies' room. The conversation had been a surprise. I had not realized word of the explosion had reached so far. How many more similar conversations would I endure before the ship docked in England? And, once there, how many more people would have heard the news? I didn't know how many times I could bear to recount the experience.

By the time I placed my hand on the wooden washroom door and pushed, my face was hot and flushed and I felt on the verge of tears. However, as soon as the door opened, all thoughts of the conversation with Lady Dixon rushed out of my head. Someone was crying.

"Hello?" I poked my head around the door, not wanting to startle an already fragile woman. As I peered around, I recognized the profile of Ruby Stratton hunched over the marble sinks, tears pouring freely from her eyes.

She jumped back, wiping madly at her eyes.

"I'm being silly," she said, shaking her head. "Don't worry about me."

I hadn't even realized Ruby had left the table. Of course, I'd been rather distracted by Lady Dixon's interrogation. Had Ruby and Colonel Stratton fought again? Or had there been a continuation of the argument they'd had in their cabin just before dinner?

When Ruby looked up, she paused for a few seconds, and then seemed to recognize me from the table. She lunged forward all at once and gripped my forearm, her fingers wrapping so tightly I was certain she'd leave a bruise.

"I fear for my life," she said in a harsh whisper, the giddy tone at the table entirely absent from her voice.

"Why do you say that?" I asked, trying to rationalize the flirtatious woman at the table with the terrified creature before me. It felt as though she were split into two entirely different people.

She breathed heavily, her wide eyes assessing me. She smelled strongly of alcohol, though I didn't remember seeing her drink much more than a glass of wine at dinner. However, I also hadn't noticed her leave, so there was no telling what else I'd missed. Ruby opened her mouth as if she wanted to say something, but then shook her head and pursed her red-stained lips together.

"It's the wine and the isolation of the ship," she said,

smoothing her hair back with her hand. "I am not as accustomed as some to life at sea. I'm going silly. I'll be fine in the morning."

She smiled at me, looking half-crazed, wiped once again at her eyes, and pushed past me. Had I not been so shaken by the dinner conversation, perhaps I would have had the energy to stop her and insist she explain herself, but as it was, I let her leave. If she'd been making use of the open bar prior to the start of dinner, there was a great chance Ruby was drunk. Which could have been the reason she and the Colonel had been fighting. Being a strict army man, perhaps he found it difficult to be married to such a silly thing as Ruby.

I washed my hands in the cold water and checked my scar in the mirror. From the front, the makeup still covered it nicely, but at certain angles, it looked jagged and fresh. Sometimes, I could still feel the hot flash of shrapnel slicing across my face, the warm blood pouring down my neck. I washed up again, not quite ready to leave the ladies room, patted cold water on my flushed neck, and shook my hands dry.

Outside the washroom, a hallway ran in either direction, large windows looking out onto the deck below and the ocean. A left would take me towards the smoking room and then towards the back of the ship, a right would lead back to the dining room. I didn't feel entirely ready to face the curiosity of Jane, the judgment of Lady Dixon, or the sympathy of the Worthings. And now, I especially didn't feel equipped to heap Ruby Stratton's problems onto the pile of my own. With all of that weighing heavily on my mind, I considered taking a left. However, I also didn't want to give anyone reason to believe I was upset, though I was. I stood outside the ladies room, paralyzed with indecision, when suddenly a man approached me.

He had a tan face and a prominent chin that would have been handsome had it not been for the pencil-thin black mustache he sported. It gave him a sinister look, and seeing him move towards me left an uneasy feeling in my stomach.

"I have been observing you," the man said, a slight French accent discernible in his voice.

I blinked several times before answering, unsure how I was supposed to respond. The man had been following me? For how long? Since boarding the ship, or had it been happening on land, as well?

"My name is Achilles Prideaux," he said. "Unravelling secrets is a major part of my profession, and I sense you have a rather important one."

"I do not have any secrets," I said, stepping to the side to move around him. The hallway had emptied, so I was alone with the strange man, and I suddenly wished I'd asked Mrs. Worthing to accompany me to the ladies' room, as women so often do. Achilles Prideaux followed my movement, blocking my path, and stepped close enough that I could hear his whisper.

"I also detect lies, Mademoiselle. Your secret is not unlike the bomb that gave you that scar. One day, it will go off and you will find yourself in great danger. I can be of assistance to you."

My hand flew to my cheek before I could stop myself. He had been observing me. At least enough to know about the bomb, and my scar. I smoothed down the fabric of my dress and straightened up, pulling my shoulders back. "I do not require your assistance, sir."

Achilles Prideaux raised his eyebrows at me, but stepped

back and waved his arm, directing me down the hallway towards the dining room. He tipped his head as I passed, bowing deeply. I rushed away from him without a second look.

How much did the man truly know about me? I liked to consider myself adept at deception, but Achilles Prideaux, a perfect stranger, had guessed that I was caught up in a lie. Perhaps, I was more transparent than I believed. And if he was close to discovering my secret, how long would it be before the others caught on and I lost everything I'd been working towards?

The sight of my companions at the dinner table brought the swirl of questions and doubts in my mind to a stop. They were talking amongst themselves—Ruby still smiling broadly at the Captain while he and Dr. Rushforth spoke animatedly about something, Mr. and Mrs. Worthing bent across my empty seat to hear whatever Lady Dixon was saying, Colonal Stratton still eating—and it was clear none of them suspected a thing. Achilles Prideaux, if that was his true identity, had probably been nothing more than a bored passenger eavesdropping on gossip and trying his best to get a rise out of me. He'd likely been repeating similar lines to every person who walked in or out of the ladies room. In fact, that would explain why Ruby Stratton had been in such a fit when I'd entered the washroom. The man had probably fooled her into believing he knew all of her secrets, as well, and threatened to expose them. Nothing would come of it, I was sure. I'd been momentarily fooled by a con artist, nothing more.

As I neared the table, the Worthings hushed and turned towards me, and the previously chatty table fell into an awkward lull. Immediately I knew they had been talking about me. Of course they had; the only reason everyone had danced around the topic of the explosion before was because I had been at the table. As soon as I'd left, it had given Mrs. Worthing the opportunity to gossip openly about my tragedy. I couldn't blame her. Had the tragedy not been my own, I would have been telling everyone, as well. Jane Dixon seemed to be the only person at the table willing to admit the obvious.

"I've just heard the rest of your story, and I am even more impressed with you than before," she said, her bright eyes glassy and somber. "You are very brave to bear up so well under such tragic circumstances. Was the madman who threw the explosive into the car ever captured?"

I thanked the young girl, and shrugged my shoulders. "I am not sure."

"You haven't followed the story?" she asked, eyes wide with astonishment.

I could tell what she was thinking. My family had perished in that vehicle. Wouldn't I want to know what had become of their murderer? The truth was that I didn't want to know. I understood that the violence had been political, because of my father's position in government. Beyond that, I preferred not to dwell on the past but to look to the future, and I said as much to Jane.

With my return, the conversation turned to more mundane topics, and I was free to sit in silence the remainder of the evening. Talking so openly about the explosion had brought back the memories in full force, and I did my best to fight them back. I couldn't allow myself to be overwhelmed by the tragedy in public. Achilles Prideaux's warning—though most likely a lie—had reminded me that there was too much at stake, narrow straits I could only navigate by keeping my wits. One misspoken word or moment of weakness, and even the kindly, guileless Worthings could guess certain truths I wished to conceal.

LYING in my cabin later that night, moonlight coming through the porthole in a single spotlight on the floor, I grabbed the chain of the locket I always wore around my neck and pulled it free of my nightgown. The locket popped open with a familiar twist of my fingers and a small scrap of paper, yellowed with age, fell into my palm. I unfolded it twice to read the clumsy scrawl: "Help me." The message was old, written years before in a desperate plea for rescue. As always, seeing the words stirred deep memories of a childhood I wished I could forget. But no matter how much I tried, I couldn't bring myself to dispose of the locket or the message within. I slipped the piece of paper back into the locket and hid it between the thin cotton fabric of my gown. I had enough to worry about in the weeks ahead without dwelling on the past.

I fell into a troubled sleep, one plagued with long dreams I could not escape in which voices followed me, all of them repeating the same question: *what really happened in Simla?*

3

I awoke the next morning to frantic knocking on my cabin door. I grabbed my robe from the hook next to the bed and wrapped it tightly around myself. The mantel clock said it was only seven in the morning.

"Who is it?" I asked. In the back of my mind was an image of Achilles Prideaux standing on the other side of the door.

The knocking came again, louder and more frantic, and I realized it was not coming from the hallway, but from the door that separated my room from the sitting room I shared with the Worthings.

"Oh, thank heavens." I recognized Mrs. Worthing's exasperated voice and opened the door to see her standing on the other side, hand pressed to her heart. "You're alive."

"Of course I am," I said, holding the door open for her to come inside. She was breathing heavily, her hair frizzy and sticking out from under her sleep bonnet. "What made you think otherwise?"

"A woman has been murdered," she said, practically screaming.

I directed Mrs. Worthing to the chair in front of my vanity and helped her sit. Clearly, she was out of sorts. Perhaps a bad dream had awoken her, and she'd taken it for reality.

"Where is Mr. Worthing?" Her husband always seemed capable of taming her nervous energy.

"In the sitting room, acting as though nothing has happened," she said, rolling her eyes. "We are awoken to news of a murder, and you'd think we'd heard nothing more exciting than the breakfast menu."

"A woman died?" I asked, only just beginning to wonder whether there was some truth to what Mrs. Worthing was saying.

She looked at me as though I'd just asked her whether the sky was blue. "Yes, someone has died! That is what I've been saying, Rose."

"Who?"

"We don't know. That is why I woke you up. I wanted to be certain you hadn't snuck out of your cabin in the middle of the night and found yourself in trouble." She shook her head, dismissing the thought, and then reached out to stroke my good cheek. "Thank the Lord you are safe."

I patted her hand once and then peeled it off of my face. "How did you find out?"

"A crew member came to the door. You'd think the Captain would have been the one to break the news to the passengers rather than a young boy. It's an ugly errand to send a child on."

"The Captain can't really be expected to visit hundreds of rooms in a single morning," I said. "What did the crew member say?"

"He informed us a female passenger had been murdered

and to stay in our rooms until the breakfast bell." She shook her head again. "Hopefully we can eat soon. I'm famished."

Mrs. Worthing had entered my room in near hysterics thinking I'd been murdered in the night and now she was complaining of hunger. Keeping up with her was exhausting. I dropped back down onto my bed and wiped at my eyes.

"Hopefully the victim isn't anyone we know," I said.

Mrs. Worthing stilled, and I suspected she was thinking of the large number of people I'd recently lost to murder.

A commotion in the hallway brought me and Mrs. Worthing to our feet once again and racing for the door. Mr. Worthing, who according to Mrs. Worthing had been quite comfortable in the sitting room only a few minutes before, must have also deemed the shouting to be unusual because he joined us in the hallway, eyes wide and searching.

Colonel Stratton was standing in the doorway of the cabin next to mine, and his usually stern features were twisted in despair.

"Where is she?" he cried, reaching out for the crew member—a young boy, barely sixteen, with long limbs and a spotty face. The boy dodged the Colonel's thick arms and pressed himself against the far wall of the hallway.

"I don't know," he said, eyes darting around the hallway for assistance. He knotted his hands nervously in the stiff white fabric of his uniform. "Captain told me to tell the passengers in this corridor not to leave their rooms until the breakfast bell sounded."

By this point, the Colonel was shouting incoherently, drawing everyone from their rooms and into the hallway. Women in various stages of undress and men with stubbly chins and white undershirts on were gawking at the drama from their doorways. The young crew member fought for a hopeless moment to usher people back into their rooms, but then gave up, shrugging and shouting, "Stay in your rooms until the breakfast bell." Then, having technically completed his duty to tell everyone the Captain's order, he darted through the crowd and around the corner, leaving chaos in his wake.

"Where is my wife?" the Colonel shouted after the young boy.

Mr. Worthing stepped forward and grabbed the large man by the shoulders, shaking him. If it hadn't been for Colonel Stratton's despair, the sight would almost have been comical—Mr. Worthing's thin fingers trying to wrap around the dense muscle of Colonel Stratton.

"Colonel!" Mr. Worthing said loudly. The word had the effect of a bucket of cold water. The Colonel straightened up, and looked into Mr. Worthing's face, blinking several times slowly. "You are making a scene."

"Let me make a scene then," the Colonel said, his voice a rumble of thunder, though his posture had begun to slouch considerably. "My wife is dead. You'd make a scene, too."

Mrs. Worthing gasped and slapped her hands over her mouth.

"Ruby?" I asked, stepping out from behind Mrs. Worthing. I was conscious of being dressed in nothing more than a nightgown and a robe, but I couldn't help myself.

The Colonel turned to me, assessing my lack of proper clothing for a moment, and then turned back to Mr. Worthing, acting as though I hadn't even spoken.

"Ruby is the woman who was murdered last night?" Mr. Worthing asked, taking a step backward, suddenly leery of the Colonel and his bulk. He had the right idea. Most murders were committed by a member of the family, typically a spouse, and the Colonel had the right temperament for such a violent act.

Colonel Stratton nodded solemnly, his lower lip tucked into his mouth.

"Have you seen her?" Mr. Worthing whispered, the thought too gruesome to speak at full volume.

The Colonel shook his head, and Mr. Worthing drew his eyebrows together. "Then, did the young boy tell you the deceased woman was your Ruby?"

Once again, the Colonel shook his head.

Mr. Worthing sighed and planted his hands on his hips. "Forgive me, but I don't understand. Why do you believe Mrs. Stratton to be murdered?"

"The crew boy only told us it was a woman. He wouldn't provide any other details," Mrs. Worthing said.

I could imagine her trying to pry information out of the poor boy. Between Mrs. Worthing's begging and the Colonel's shouting, he was having a rough second day at sea.

"She disappeared from the room early this morning," the Colonel said, running his fingers through the thin hair hanging on to his scalp. "She often has trouble sleeping, so I assumed she went for a walk on the deck, but now there is a woman murdered and my Ruby is still missing."

His voice cracked on her name, and his square face was made even more square by the tightening of his jaw. The Colonel was fighting back tears. He shook his head and composed himself.

"We will find your Ruby," Mr. Worthing said. "She was probably on deck when the body was discovered and directed to the smoking room or dining room to wait until the breakfast bell."

Colonel Stratton didn't disagree, but I could see that he didn't believe Mr. Worthing.

"Let's go back inside until the bell," Mrs. Worthing whispered in my ear. "The men will handle the Colonel."

Mrs. Worthing lounged back on my bed, her arm thrown over her eyes to block the morning sun pouring through the porthole, while I reapplied my makeup, covering the scar that ran across my cheek. Immediately after the accident, the doctor had told me to keep the area clean as it healed, but as soon as the wound closed, I'd covered it with cream and powder.

"Do you think there is any truth to the Colonel's claims? Could Ruby Stratton have found herself in harm's way?" Mrs. Worthing asked, faux horror dripping from every word. Though Mrs. Worthing liked to pretend she was a well-mannered, high-class woman, her love of gossip revealed her heart. I had no doubt her concern for Mrs. Stratton was real, but she found too great an enjoyment in discussing the topic for it to be entirely proper.

I fear for my life. Those were the words Ruby had confided to me in the ladies room less than twelve hours before. Had it been only twelve hours? I'd left dinner confident that Ruby had been spooked by a mean trick played by Achilles Prideaux—the same trick he'd tried to play on me —but had it been a trick? Or had Mr. Prideaux known something about Ruby that lead to her demise? And if so, what did that mean for my own secret?

"I don't know what to believe," I said, the answer as vague and truthful as I could manage.

When the breakfast bell finally rang, I was desperate for a break from Mrs. Worthing's company. She talked incessantly, barely giving me a moment to sit with my own thoughts, of which I had many. The chief of which was how to discover who the murdered woman was. I prayed it was anyone but Ruby Stratton—not only because I knew Ruby as well as anyone could know someone after one dinner together, but also because her death would make me a likely next target, assuming the murderer was Achilles Prideaux.

The passengers moved through the hallway in slow groups, everyone suspicious, but doing their best to act as if nothing were wrong. I navigated around them quickly, losing Mrs. Worthing when she forced Mr. Worthing back into their stateroom to change out of his dinner jacket and into a navy blazer.

"This is a ship, not the embassy," she scolded him. Mr. Worthing had only been retired two days, and already seemed to be missing his routine. "We won't be just a minute, Rose."

I breathed in the fresh air on the Pomenade Deck greedily. I hadn't anticipated how claustrophobic the cabin would make me feel, and I promised myself in that moment to spend as much time out of my cabin as possible. Assuming, of course, I was not in any immediate danger. Being out of my room and away from the wild theories of Mrs. Worthing, the idea of Ruby Stratton being the murdered woman felt silly. Colonel Stratton had simply been overreacting, and trapped as we were in our rooms, his fear had consumed us all. And it wasn't just me benefitting from the effects of the fresh sea air. Everyone seemed in better spirits, almost as if the murder hadn't happened at all.

A woman in a white dress and apron brought me a steaming cup of tea, and I thanked her, wrapping my hands around the warm cup and looking out into the ocean. India was no longer visible on the horizon, and turquoise sea surrounded the ship in all directions like a moving island. The thought of isolation should have scared me, but fear was not an emotion I felt capable of just then. With India slipping ever more into the background and on a steady course for my new life in London, I felt free. The *RMS Star of India* ripped through the water and foamy waves churned and then disappeared back into the ocean, taking all of my worries with them.

When I heard the Worthings walking towards where I stood at the ship's railing, Mrs. Worthing hysterical about one thing or another, I was hardly able to even muster the energy to turn around and see what she was going on about. But I did, and I was met with wide, tear-stained cheeks and words too garbled with tears for me to understand.

"What has happened?" I asked, looking from a sobbing Mrs. Worthing to a stiff, stoic Mr. Worthing.

Mr. Worthing opened his mouth to talk, but Mrs. Worthing held him off with a wave of her hand still gripping a soaked handkerchief. She wanted to deliver the news herself. She tried again, but I was left open-mouthed and more confused than concerned.

"Has the news reached you all yet?"

Dr. Rushforth was walking towards our small group, his hand clutching the railing as if he were afraid he would fall overboard.

"What news?" I asked.

Dr. Rushforth leaned forward and whispered, forcing the Worthings and myself to lean forward conspiratorially. "I just spoke to the Captain and he informed me the woman who was murdered on deck last night was—"

Not to be outdone, Mrs. Worthing broke into a sudden and rather loud sob, effectively interrupting Dr. Rushforth. Once all eyes were on her, she reached out and grabbed my shoulders, drawing me into her. "The Colonel was right. Ruby Stratton is dead."

4

S uddenly, the wind on Deck A felt too cold, and I wished I'd grabbed the shawl I had packed in my steamer trunk. A shiver ran through me.

"Exactly," Dr. Rushforth said, agreeing with Mrs. Worthing's rather blunt take on the situation and shaking his head from side to side. "It is truly horrible news, isn't it?"

"The Captain told you this, Dr. Rushforth?" I asked, head tilted in confusion. How had he gained access to such private information?

He nodded, his features made even more pointed by the forced frown pulling the lower half of his face into a point. "I went to the bridge to see him once I heard the news in case I could be of any assistance. Of course, my expertise is in healing the living, and Mrs. Stratton had, unfortunately, been dead for some time."

"Did you see her body?" Mrs. Worthing asked, a handkerchief pressed to her nose.

He shook his head and looked out over the water, a dark expression on his face.

"How did she...die?" Mr. Worthing asked, the words

coming out as if he wasn't entirely sure he wanted to speak them aloud. The situation was beyond the realm of normal day-to-day etiquette, but everyone seemed to universally understand that being too interested in the gruesome details of a murder was not exactly polite. Still, everyone leaned in a little closer in anticipation of Dr. Rushforth's answer.

"I did not ask," said Dr. Rushforth. "Once the Captain told me I was not needed, I left immediately so he could oversee the investigation."

"Such a shame," Mr. Worthing said. "The poor Colonel must be devastated. Has he been informed?"

Dr. Rushforth pulled his mouth into a tight line. "You overestimate my familiarity with the situation, sir. I have no knowledge of the issue beyond the identity of the victim."

"Of course. Of course. Do excuse me. We are all rather out of sorts this morning. I am not myself without break-fast." Mr. Worthing busied himself staring at his thumbs and tapping his foot.

"I can't believe this has happened on our second day at sea," Mrs. Worthing said, making a tisk in the back of her throat. "It will certainly put a damper on the rest of the voyage."

"Ruby Stratton's trip has certainly been spoiled," I said, unable to hold my tongue. The woman's death felt oddly personal after our run-in in the ladies' room the night before. She had confided in me, telling me she feared for her life, even if moments later she had tried to downplay her words. I should have told someone, warned someone to keep an eye on her. Instead, I'd allowed myself to be distracted by Achilles Prideaux's threat. I could have prevented her murder.

No, I couldn't think that way. My hand played no part in

the death of Ruby; therefore, I was not to blame. The only person at fault was her murderer.

"Rose!" Mrs. Worthing chastised. "Now is not the time for jokes."

"I don't believe it was a joke, beloved," Mr. Worthing said, trying to calm his wife. "She was only saying that we have not been nearly as inconvenienced as Mrs. Stratton. We should be grateful we have our lives."

Mrs. Worthing huffed her displeasure. Since becoming acquainted with the Worthings, I had stayed rather quiet, leading Mrs. Worthing to believe me a valued confidante and fellow gossiper. Partly because I didn't wish to say anything to offend the people who were seeing me halfway around the world, and partly because Mrs. Worthing's lack of social graces seemed unimportant in the face of the trauma I'd endured in Simla. Now, though, with Ruby Stratton's body being stowed away like cargo, going cold in some unused room in the belly of the ship, it felt wrong to let anyone diminish whatever horror she had endured in the last moments of her life by suggesting her death to be little more than an inconvenience.

"I think I'll go for a walk before breakfast," I said.

Mrs. Worthing, usually so hesitant to let me wander off, gave no indication she would miss my company.

"I'll come along, too," Dr. Rushforth said. "If you do not mind, of course?"

"Of course not."

Truth was, I did mind. A tumultuous storm of emotions was swirling inside my mind, and I needed time alone to sort through them. But that would clearly have to wait until later.

"I did not mean to impose myself on you," Dr. Rushforth whispered as we strolled leisurely towards the stern of the boat. The deck was wide enough to allow five people—six if they were all rather thin—to walk alongside one another, but still Dr. Rushforth chose to hug my side, the fabric of his suit jacket brushing against my fingers. "I hope I have not mistaken your feelings on the matter, but I must say I'm not keen on the idea of being left alone with the Worthings."

Despite everything that had happened that morning, I smiled slightly. "You have perfectly understood my feelings. The Worthings are not bad people, but they would not be my first choice of travelling companions."

"It seems as if you were left with little choice in that matter," he said somberly.

I nodded. "Without that silly couple, I would have been quite alone in the world."

"I am sorry for your loss," he said. "As an army doctor, I saw my fair share of violent death, but I never lost anyone close to me in such a manner, and certainly not all at once. It must have been unbearable."

"I would not wish it on my worst enemy," I said.

The morning sun cast the ocean in brilliant shades of orange and yellow that changed as the waves broke around the ship, and we paused at the railing to admire the view.

Dr. Rushforth was facing the ocean, but he cast a quick glance in my direction. "Certainly, a woman as lovely as you has no true enemies."

I was aware of the fact that the Doctor was flirting with me, quite openly, as well. I raised an eyebrow at him. "You'd be surprised."

"I suppose so," he said with a smirk. "Would you like to accompany me to the café?"

Most everyone was headed to the first-class dining room for breakfast, so the café was empty. Dr. Rushforth ordered one finger of brandy, raising an eyebrow from the young waitress, and a plate of scrambled eggs while I ordered an orange juice.

"It is only breakfast, but I am already in need of some invigorating," he said in explanation for his pre-noonday drink. "And please feel free to order yourself something. This will all be going to my tab."

The Worthings were paying for my ticket as I wouldn't have any money until I received my inheritance, and I had to assume they wouldn't appreciate me wracking up a bill at the café when meals were included in the cost of the ticket.

"Really, I'm fine," I said, though my stomach growled.

Despite my assurances, Dr. Rushforth ordered me a fresh pastry to accompany my juice.

"How long do you think Mrs. Stratton's death will be making news on the ship?" he asked as he swirled his liquor. "Two days?"

The brazen way he addressed the topic made me nearly choke on my orange juice. "Surely longer than that?"

He shrugged. "People do not wish to dwell on bad news, no matter how sensational. Would you like to make a wager?"

"A lady does not gamble," I said. And certainly not about such a macabre topic.

He leaned in, the smell of brandy thick on his breath. "It will be our little secret. I give it four days."

I used my knife and fork to slice off a bit of the cinnamon pastry and placed it in my mouth, chewing slowly and swallowing. "What is at stake?"

Dr. Rushforth clapped his hands and leaned back in his chair. "I took you for a good sport the moment I saw you, and you have not disappointed. How about, if I win we share another meal together at the café? Preferably dinner."

"A date?"

He shrugged, his mouth quirking upwards.

"And what do I win?" I asked.

"The great privilege of besting me," he said. "It is rarely done."

Dr. Rushforth did not strike me as a particularly hand-some man, and I had no intention of finding myself in a relationship anytime soon—not with the incident in Simla so fresh in my memory and so much to do once the ship docked in London. But despite the very clear age gap between us, Dr. Rushforth made for interesting company, and I was in no position to turn that down. "I think people will be discussing the finer details long past when we dock in Aden," I said.

He raised his eyebrows and lifted his glass. "May the best man win."

I touched his glass with my own. "May the best *woman* win."

Dr. Rushforth smiled, and we slipped into an easy conversation about his education at Oxford, and his time in the war.

"I was just a child when the war ended," I told him. "Barely fifteen."

Dr. Rushforth pretended to plug his ears. "You make me feel like an ancient artifact," he joked. "You seem far beyond your years, then."

The waitress came over to refill our drinks—Dr. Rush-forth accepted a second brandy glass—and then she leaned forward. "Forgive me, but I was serving in the first-class dining room last night. Were you not at the same table as the woman who was murdered?"

I looked up at the girl for the first time. She had red hair that hugged her face in tight ringlets. She'd pulled it back into a low bun, probably required in her line of work, and wore a white knee-length dress in a crisp cotton with a matching white apron.

Dr. Rushforth and I looked at one another, neither of us sure exactly how we should answer, but the waitress didn't seem to require our response. She'd recognized us, and her question had merely been a transitional sentence to begin the conversation, not an actual inquiry.

"I only wondered if there is any clue as to who could have committed the crime," she said. "Since you are her friends. All of the staff are a little anxious, as you can imagine. We interact with all of the passengers, and aren't awarded the same privilege of locking ourselves away in our room for safety. I'd like to disembark this ship in London, if you know what I mean."

"I don't believe we will have a repeat of Mrs. Stratton's murder, if that's what you're insinuating," Dr. Rushforth said.

"How can you be certain?" the woman asked, eyes wide.

"I can't, but the odds are in your favor. It is very unlikely that multiple murders would happen on the same ship on the same voyage."

"I'm sure Mrs. Stratton, as you've called her, would have said the same about her chances of being murdered last night when I saw her mingling with the bartender near midnight," the waitress said, not at all convinced by Dr. Rushforth's logic. "It was clear she had no fear, yet her life was hours from being ended."

Dr. Rushforth's face pulled into a tight frown, and he quickly dismissed the waitress by requesting a fresh brandy, though his was no more than three minutes old.

"The staff here have no shame," he grumbled as he downed his glass. "And she told such tales, too. Talking of Ruby at the bar until midnight? Nonsense."

"How do you know she was lying?" I asked. The waitress had seemed perfectly sincere to me. I was fast asleep by midnight and had no knowledge of Ruby's movements after dinner. How did Dr. Rushforth know so much about her whereabouts?

He opened his mouth and then closed it, shaking his head. "It just feels untrue. Ruby didn't make a habit of mingling with the lower classes, not after marrying the Colonel."

Again, I tilted my head to the side and stared at him. "I'm sorry, but I was under the impression you only met Ruby last night at dinner. Were you acquainted with her prior to boarding the ship?"

He stared at me blankly for a moment and then rushed into an animated head shake. "No, I'd never laid eyes on her before yesterday, but I've known enough high-class women in my life to know they wouldn't waste their time with staff while on a ship stuffed to the brim with high-ranking government officials, famous celebrities of the stage and screen, and men in uniform."

I nodded, trying my best to accept his explanation. "And you mentioned her marriage to the Colonel..." I said, trailing off, the question not yet fully formed.

"Ruby was significantly younger than the Colonel, as I'm sure you noticed," he said, tapping a rhythm on the table with his fingers. "And I can't be the only one who picked up on her lack of dinner etiquette. It is clear the Colonel married Ruby not because of her social status, but because of her beauty. And rarely is a low-born girl excited about the prospect of returning to her roots when she has been shown the grandeur of the highest tree-tops."

I had picked up on all the same things he had mentioned, but I supposed I had fancied myself a keener observer of the human character than most other people. It hadn't crossed my mind that Dr. Rushforth could have come to the same conclusions as I had.

"Have I satisfied your questions?" he asked, pushing his glass to the center of the table and standing up with an amused smile. "Or will the interrogation continue?"

My curiosity had not truly been satisfied in the least, but it was clear I would be pushing my luck by asking him any more questions for the time being.

"An interrogation? My, for an army man, you certainly are sensitive," I teased. "Can a woman not ask simple questions?"

"A woman can," he said, offering me his arm as we moved to join our fellow passengers at breakfast. "But those were not simple questions and I suspect you are no ordinary woman."

I looked out at the ocean as we walked down the deck. Dr. Rushforth truly had no idea how unordinary I was.

5

The main dining room was awash in shades of red and blue as the morning sun shone through the stained-glass skylights. Diners dressed in neutral-colored tea gowns and suits stooped over their fried eggs and toast, and talked in hushed tones about what the day would hold and what had already transpired.

"How do you think they make so many eggs?" Mr. Worthing asked as he sliced into the soft yolk of his third egg and let it bleed across his plate and into his toast. "The kitchen onboard must be massive."

"I'm sure the Captain would provide a tour if you were interested in one," Dr. Rushforth said.

"Do you think so?" Mr. Worthing asked, a childlike excitement bubbling out of him.

"Absolutely. He's a very friendly man."

"Why waste time looking at a kitchen when you could explore the indoor swimming pool or the Turkish bath?" Mrs. Worthing asked, sipping on her coffee and leaving dark maroon lipstick stains on the rim of her mug.

"This ship is more than just amenities, dear," Mr.

Worthing said. "It is a feat of engineering and technology. A signpost for human advancement in the face of great odds."

"We've had boats for hundreds of years," she responded flatly, not allowing herself to be tangled up in Mr. Worthing's enthusiasm.

"I'll join you on a tour of the ship and maybe I'll find out what happened to my mother's brooch," Lady Dixon said. Since I'd known her, her mouth had been pulled into a near-constant frown, but today it looked especially sour.

"Have you misplaced your jewelry?" Mrs. Worthing asked.

Lady Dixon barked out a laugh. "Misplaced? No. The brooch was stolen, I'm sure of it."

Mrs. Worthing gasped. "Are you certain?"

"Well, I certainly didn't lose it. I've carried the brooch with me since my dear, sweet mother left this Earth twenty years ago, and it wasn't until I stepped onto this ship that it went missing."

"What time did you last see the brooch?" I asked.

The old woman did not seem particularly interested in talking to me, but her desire to complain overrode her disdain. "I don't make a habit of tracking the points in the day at which I notice my belongings being present. I do, however, remember when I noticed the brooch missing. Last night after dinner, I reached into my bag and noticed the brooch was no longer pinned to the handle."

"You kept it pinned on the outside of your bag?"

"If you're insinuating that the brooch could have fallen off of my bag, then I'll beg you to save your breath," Lady Dixon said, turning her hawk-like eyes on me. "I check the clasp every morning, and it was functioning perfectly yesterday morning."

Lady Dixon's insistence that a brooch she had carried for

twenty years and that had belonged to her mother for who knew how many years before that was not capable of breaking seemed completely in character for her. She would have believed the sun incapable of shining if she'd commanded it to be overcast.

"I will help you look for it after breakfast," Mrs. Worthing said, patting Lady Dixon's hand. "I'm sure we will find it around here somewhere. Have you checked with the janitorial staff? Perhaps there is a lost and found area where someone turned it in."

Lady Dixon didn't seem convinced, but she at least seemed tired of talking about the matter. Instead, she swatted her niece's elbows off the table, and told her to sit up. "Really, Jane. Do you want to be a hunchback? My spine isn't this straight because of years of slouching."

As breakfast was winding down, Mr. Worthing thought to order a plate of pancakes for Colonel Stratton.

"I'm certain he isn't hungry, dear," Mrs. Worthing said. "His wife just died. If I had been the one who was murdered, I hope you wouldn't be scarfing down a full breakfast a few hours after learning the news."

"It's more about the gesture than the actual food," Mr. Worthing said. "He was upset this morning, and I'm sure his devastation has only grown now that Ruby's identity has been confirmed."

Mr. Worthing directed our waiter to bring an extra breakfast plate, and as he went into unnecessary detail on the fluffiness of the pancakes and requested that there be exactly three extra cups of maple syrup on the side, a dark figure lurking at the edge of the room caught my attention.

Medium-height and broad-shouldered, the man was wearing a dark suit, an unseasonably long coat, and a hat pulled low over his eyes. He stayed close to the wall, his face turned away from the tables. He looked like a man who didn't want to be recognized, but his black cap toe oxfords gave him away. Colonel Stratton had made enough trips to and from the table at dinner the night before for me to become familiar with his shoes.

I snuck away while Mr. Worthing was trying to outline the plan by which he could deliver food to Colonel Stratton and Mrs. Worthing could help Lady Dixon find her missing brooch, and they would still meet up in time for their badminton game at ten. Somehow, while the Colonel was shouting about his wife being murdered, Mr. Worthing had found time to schedule a game with the middle-aged couple in the cabin across the hall from ours.

"I will meet you on the deck in half an hour," he said. Mr. Worthing's arms were loaded down with a travel cup of orange juice and a massive plate of pancakes with precisely three sauce cups of maple syrup balanced on the rim.

"We won't be done in half an hour," Lady Dixon cried. Her niece Jane was leaning against a beam that ran from the floor into the ceiling two-stories above, nervously running her hand along the hem of her pink drop-waist dress with a white peter pan collar. "We have to search the entire deck. That will take at least an hour."

"What if we meet on the deck in an hour?" Mrs. Worthing amended.

Mr. Worthing nodded, and then wrinkled his forehead. "Where on the deck?"

"Near the café," Mrs. Worthing said.

"Which café?"

"Honestly, dear, how could you not have noticed that giant veranda? It shades half of the starboard side."

"You mean port," Mr. Worthing corrected.

"So, you do know which café I'm referring to, then?"

I did not stick around to learn where Mr. and Mrs. Worthing were going to meet up on the deck. Colonel Stratton was slipping through the back door of the dining room and I didn't want to lose him in the departing breakfast crowd.

"I'll see you in the room for lunch," I said over my shoulder, eyes trained on the black clad figure of Colonel Stratton.

Despite everyone whispering about Ruby Stratton's murder—who could have done it, how she must have died, where on the ship it happened—no one paid her husband any mind as he moved amongst them towards the bridge.

A narrow flight of stairs, painted white and labeled with a 'Crew Only' sign, were set into the far corner of the lobby just outside the dining room, and Colonel Stratton took the stairs two at a time. I followed behind him, moving up the stairs as quietly and as quickly as I could in my heels. I stopped in the middle of the stairwell, far enough down that Colonel Stratton could not see me from his place on the landing, but close enough that I could hear the four solid knocks he landed on the door at the top of the stairs.

"Open the door, you slimy weasel." Colonel Stratton was pounding on the door with both fists now. It took several more seconds before the door finally opened.

"What in the name of—" Captain Croft's voice was deep and shaken, but the Colonel's shouting washed over everything, echoing off the metal walls.

"My wife died on your ship."

"Colonel, I know you have suffered a tremendous loss," Captain Croft said evenly, trying to reason with the enraged man.

But reason had no place in Colonel Stratton's mind anymore. He was incensed. "You made eyes at her right in front of me, and then let her die on you ship. Something should have been done. There should have been more security. A woman shouldn't have been able to sneak out of her room and wander the ship by herself," he yelled.

"You are paying guests, not inmates," the Captain said. "I can't force anyone to stay in their rooms if they do not wish to do so. I am terribly sorry for your loss, and we are doing all we can to bring the culprit to justice."

"Doing all you can," the Colonel repeated with a scoff. "No one cares about my wife. Not now she is dead. You cared about her plenty last night, wooing her with talk of your travels and the great ships you've commanded. I've commanded armies!"

"You are distraught, Colonel. I sympathize with your loss and your pain, but if you don't calm down, I will have to call security to come and take care of you."

"I want financial restitution!"

"Excuse me?" Captain Croft asked.

"You said yourself that my wife was a paying guest. She did not live to receive her money's worth, and I would like it returned to me."

"I can't do that—" the Captain began to say, but he was interrupted by the Colonel's harsh whisper.

"Perhaps you were my wife's murderer. You clearly took a fancy to her at dinner last night, and perhaps she refused to return your advances. And perhaps that made you angry."

"Hey now," Captain Croft protested.

Colonel Stratton continued as if the Captain hadn't spoken at all. "And perhaps a little bit of money would keep me quiet about the whole thing. A captain accused of murdering one of his passengers certainly wouldn't find much more work, not once the news began to spread,"

"That is quite enough!" Captain Croft said, having finally reached his breaking point. "I have indulged this for far too long. I understand you are grieving a major loss, but I can't allow you to make such serious and baseless accusations against my character. I never touched your wife—for *any* reason."

I heard the Colonel inhale as if ready to respond, but just as he did, wrapped up in the heated exchange as I was, I forgot myself and my foot slipped from the stair. The noise was slight, but it echoed off the walls, and I heard the two men go silent.

I was left with two options: run and hope I could make it down the stairs and around the corner before being detected, or stay put and try to make an excuse. I chose the latter.

Stomping up the remainder of the stairs as obviously as I could, I smiled as Colonel Stratton looked down at me. From my angle several stairs below him, his square jaw looked sharper and more threatening. And with his face as red as it was, I began to wonder whether I shouldn't have run away. Still, I did my best to keep calm.

"Mr. Worthing has prepared you a breakfast plate and is on his way to your room as we speak," I said. "I saw you heading up these stairs from my table at breakfast"—this distance would have provided enough time for the two men's conversation to have been almost at its conclusion by the time I would have travelled from my seat to my current position on the stairs—"and thought I would come and warn you."

The two men stared down at me blankly, unsure what to do with my sudden interruption. Captain Croft looked half-prepared to continue shouting at Colonel Stratton, and

Colonel Stratton looked as though he had half a mind to shove me down the stairs.

"Good morning...Miss Beckingham, is it?" Captain Croft said, slightly unsure.

I nodded. "You have a good memory, Captain."

The Colonel still hadn't responded to my mention of breakfast, and I didn't have any other reason to remain on the stairs, so I quickly bid them both farewell, and moved down the stairs and back into the now empty dining room. Servers in bright white uniforms were collecting plates and sweeping floors, and none of them paid me any attention at all, so I leaned against the far wall closest to the starboard deck.

I couldn't be sure whether either the Captain or the Colonel had believed my hastily thought out excuse, but that didn't seem to matter either way. At worst, they both thought I was too nosy for my own good. Unless, of course, Colonel Stratton's theory had been correct. If the Captain's advances towards Ruby Stratton had been spurned and he'd become angry enough to kill her, I could be in danger, as well. The Captain wouldn't want that information getting out, and unlike Colonel Stratton, I wouldn't be bought off.

That was another point of interest. Why would the Colonel be willing to accept money to remain quiet about his own wife's murder? Wouldn't he want her murderer brought to justice? For a man meant to be grieving his wife, he had seemed awfully concerned about his bottom line.

I leaned forward so I could see the stairwell through the dining room doorway. Colonel Stratton was just reaching the bottom of the stairs, his face and neck as red as a ripe tomato. Clearly, he had done a good deal more arguing after my departure. What I wouldn't have given to know what the two men had discussed. The Colonel glanced around the lobby, eyeing a few giggling women as they walked from one side of the deck to the other, arms linked. He lowered his hat over his eyes, shoved his hands in his pockets, and stalked away.

"Oh, Rose, there you are."

I turned to see Mrs. Worthing and Lady Dixon walking towards me, Jane trailing behind them, dragging her feet along the wood floor.

"You can help us search for Lady Dixon's missing brooch," Mrs. Worthing said.

I had no desire to help Lady Dixon with anything, as she had taken an instant and rather severe dislike to me, but I didn't have an excuse. Mrs. Worthing knew I didn't have any plans, as she had chastised me for being anti-social the night before when I'd told her I intended to do little more than lounge in one of the wicker deck chairs and read for the three-week voyage. And all of my quick thinking had been spent when I'd been caught by Colonel Stratton only a few minutes before on the stairs to the bridge.

"Of course," I said, trying to muster as much cheer as I could.

Lady Dixon still offered me a scowl, and she and Mrs. Worthing charged ahead, leading Jane and I through the dining room and out onto the deck.

The day was bright and warm, with a crosswind that made all the men hold onto their hats and the women flatten down their skirts.

"Perhaps your brooch blew off deck," Mrs. Worthing joked as her hair came loose from its twist and blew around her face. Her smile faltered when she noticed Lady Dixon was not even remotely amused. "Of course, I'm only teasing. We will find it, I'm sure."

"You hear such horrible tales of the many things that go

missing on a ship like this. Criminals steal whatever they can find in international waters, and then escape into a new country before they can be prosecuted. It's horrible." Lady Dixon clacked her tongue and shook her head, clutching her bag a little tighter to her chest than normal.

"There are downsides to travelling by ship," Mrs. Worthing agreed. "Though, you meet all manner of interesting people. For instance, we have become rather fast friends, haven't we?"

Lady Dixon nodded her head noncommittally and straightened her shoulders so she stood slightly taller than Mrs. Worthing, as if her height alone could put the other woman in her place. "We ought to pay more mind to our surroundings and less to conversation," she said.

Mrs. Worthing ran a finger over her lips to zip them, and set her eyes on the ground, searching from side to side in case the brooch happened to fall from Lady Dixon's bag and roll under a deck chair.

"Do you remember when Lady Dixon last had her brooch?" I whispered to Jane.

She shook her head, but otherwise remained silent, her lips pressed resolutely together.

"This seems like a rather pointless endeavor," I said, leaning down to ensure the two women in front of us didn't overhear our conversation. "We won't find such a small brooch on a ship this large."

"The brooch was actually quite large," Jane answered, holding her hand up, her thumb and forefinger forming a shape roughly the size of an apple.

"Wow. If it is as large as you say, then she would have heard it hit the ground had it fallen from her bag," I said.

Jane flattened her lips and stared straight ahead, her eyes fixated on the back of Lady Dixon's gray head.

"People are whispering about the Strattons and a possible extra-marital affair," Mrs. Worthing said to Lady Dixon, her hand pressed to the side of her mouth, but her voice at normal volume. "Do you think there is any truth to it?"

"It wouldn't surprise me in the slightest. Mrs. Stratton made no secret about her appreciation for male company," Lady Dixon said. "Why Colonel Stratton ever married her is beyond me. A high-ranking army man marrying a girl from a low-class family doesn't seem to make any sense. What did he gain from the match besides a pretty face?"

"A pretty face is quite important to some men," Mrs. Worthing said.

"Yes, but if death hadn't stolen her beauty first, age would have. And then what would he have been left with?"

The question was open-ended, but I understood that Lady Dixon believed Ruby Stratton offered up nothing beyond her appearance. I also gathered from the conversation that Lady Dixon knew more about Ruby and the Colonel than she could have gathered in a single dinner.

"Did you know the Strattons prior to boarding the ship, Jane?" I whispered, hoping Jane would open up to me. Lady Dixon treated the poor girl horribly, and I hoped she would latch on to me as a female role model and confidante if I treated her as an equal. However, she pretended as if she hadn't heard me and stepped forward so she trailed more closely behind Lady Dixon, effectively ending our covert conversation.

"Did you know the Strattons prior to boarding the ship, Lady Dixon?" I asked, repeating the question loud enough for everyone to hear.

Lady Dixon startled at my question, putting her hand on her heart and half-turning to look at me as though she'd forgotten I was there. She ran her eyes over me disapprovingly, pursed her mouth together, and then nodded. "Yes, I knew her."

"Oh my, I'm so sorry," Mrs. Worthing said. "I had no idea she was a friend of yours."

Lady Dixon held up a hand to silence Mrs. Worthing's condolences. "Mrs. Stratton was no friend of mine. She and the Colonel ran in a similar circle during the brief time Jane and I lived in Bombay. We saw them quite often at parties, but had no other contact beyond that."

Mrs. Worthing pressed a hand to the old woman's spine and patted her several times, all the while shaking her head. "Still, it must be hard to know someone you once saw at social functions has been murdered. I couldn't imagine it."

"Honestly, I'm not so surprised." Lady Dixon said the words with little emotion, her eyes still devoted to the task of finding her missing brooch.

I couldn't imagine being unsurprised at a murder. I had met all manner of unsavory people in my life, but if any of them were murdered, it would cause at least an eyebrow raise. Besides, from the little I'd seen of her, Ruby seemed friendly.

"Certainly, the news was a little shocking," Mrs. Worthing said. "Mrs. Stratton was such a sweetheart at dinner last night."

Lady Dixon laughed, though it was too sharp and brief to sound like anything but an insult. "A sweetheart, indeed. Especially if you were Dr. Rushforth or the Captain. I saw her making eyes at both of them. And right in front of the Colonel!"

"It just seemed like a bit of good fun to me," Mrs. Worthing said in defense of the dead woman.

"If you consider adultery a 'bit of good fun,' then

perhaps Jane and I ought to find a new dinner companion."
Lady Dixon lifted her chin and turned her face towards
the ocean.

"The Colonel didn't seem to mind," I said to insert
myself back into the conversation, even though it wasn't
entirely true. Colonel Stratton had just made his displeasure
with his wife's flirtatious nature quite clear when talking to
Captain Croft.

"That doesn't make it right," Lady Dixon said, refusing to
budge on her opinion of Ruby Stratton. Death usually made
people more unwilling to focus on a person's flaws, but Lady
Dixon did not allow the hurdle of death to stop her from
dragging Ruby Stratton's name through the mud. "I saw the
way she treated her poor husband, throwing herself at any
man who would have her. It was repulsive, and an embarrassment. I hope he will now find himself a true lady to
spend the rest of his days with."

"So, you think she deserved to die?" I asked.

Mrs. Worthing gasped. "Rose! Of course, no one believes
that."

Lady Dixon let out a dainty little cough, and patted her
hand across her lips. Mrs. Worthing turned to her walking
companion, eyes disbelieving.

"I do not believe she deserved to die," Lady Dixon said,
and then paused, pleased to have the attention of the entire
party. "I do, however, believe one reaps what one sows. And
Mrs. Stratton sowed mischief."

I thought that if that were the case, Lady Dixon would
one day reap an entire field of spite, but I decided not to
share this observation aloud. Lady Dixon seemed to see
everyone she met in a negative light, but she took on an
especially mean-spirited tone when talking about Ruby
Stratton. I had to wonder why. She spoke highly of the

Colonel, despite him appearing, to me, to be a large lump of a man who ate more than any person should, and was concerned about his finances hours after learning of his wife's death—not particularly attractive character traits. Colonel Stratton was closer to Lady Dixon's age than to Ruby's. Could they have carried on an affair? It seemed unlikely considering Lady Dixon's disapproval of Ruby even talking too flirtatiously to the Captain. Perhaps, rather than an affair, it was a case of unrequited love. Lady Dixon liked the Colonel, but he decided to marry a younger, more beautiful woman.

"How well did you know the Strattons?" I asked.

Lady Dixon sighed. "As I already said, I saw them at several parties while in Bombay, but never interacted with them beyond that."

"You speak on the subject of the couple with a high degree of familiarity," I said. "For someone who didn't know them well, that is."

The old woman had been staring straight ahead during our entire conversation, her black shoes slapping against the deck, but suddenly she stopped walking and whipped around, her sharp, cold eyes narrowed at me. "I am a keen observer of people. While everyone else talks and laughs and converses, I observe. I watch and I listen. I know all I will ever need to know about someone within one conversation."

"That must be a useful skill."

Lady Dixon leaned away from me and then turned on her heel to continue walking down the deck. "It has served me well, thus far."

Since leaving the hospital in Simla and connecting with the Worthings, I had been looking forward to the voyage from India to England. I was excited to be away from the pressures of everyday life. To sit back and relax in a way I had never been able to before. But now, Ruby Stratton's scared face filled my mind. Her words, hurried and frightened, repeated over and over in my ears. She had spent the last hours of her life afraid, and now she was dead. Someone had caused that fear, and as the person she had confided in, I felt it was my duty to find out who was responsible.

6

W hen Mrs. Worthing broke away from Lady Dixon's brooch search to join Mr. Worthing for their game of badminton, I took the opportunity to excuse myself and find a comfortable deck chair in a quiet corner of the ship. Several families walked by in their swimming costumes, headed for the swimming pool on one of the lower decks, and an elderly man sat in a chair on the opposite side of the deck, wrestling the wind for control of his book. The pages flapped wildly, causing him to lose his place every few minutes. He would grumble under his breath as he licked his fingers and flipped the pages. Otherwise, though, I was perfectly alone for the first time all morning, and it allowed me time to think.

The suspect list was long—nearly six-hundred passengers and two-hundred crew members were aboard the *RMS Star of India* at the time of Ruby Stratton's murder—but our dinner table the final night of Ruby's life seemed a fine place to start. At the table were eight individuals. Four of whom—myself, the Worthings, and Ruby herself—I would immediately cross off my list of suspects. Of course, I had not committed the murder. The Worthings seemed incapable of pulling off a crime of that magnitude and keeping it entirely quiet. And Ruby, herself, had to be removed from the list. If it had been a suicide, certainly one of the many people who viewed the body would have said as much. No one would have wanted to worry the rest of the passengers unnecessarily with talk of a murderer. With those four removed, I was left with Colonel Stratton, Dr. Rushforth, Lady Dixon, and Jane. Also, not to be omitted, was Captain Croft, who did not dine at the table, but visited with Ruby during the evening.

Especially after overhearing Colonel Stratton's heated exchange with Captain Croft after breakfast, I had to set my sights on him first. Not only would the Colonel have had the opportunity to murder his wife, but more than anyone, it appeared he could have had a motive. Although it had appeared he had noticed nothing beyond his plate at dinner that night, his wife's flirting had not gone unnoticed. In fact, he'd yelled at Captain Croft for making eyes at his wife. Plus, I'd heard he and Ruby arguing in their cabin earlier that afternoon, and it had been quite heated. Could Ruby's flirting have been the straw that broke the camel's back? Perhaps, the Colonel had allowed his anger to consume him, and he'd done something unforgivable to Ruby. Plus, the Colonel had been certain Ruby was the murdered woman before it had even been confirmed. The majority of people when put in that situation would choose to hope for the best until proven otherwise, but Colonel Stratton had announced to the entire corridor that his wife was dead.

There was no question that my amateur sleuthing skills would all be trained on Colonel Stratton, but now I needed to figure out how to proceed. I would not be able to simply ask the Colonel whether he had murdered his wife, and even if the questioning could be more subtle, there was no way he would consent to a conversation with me. I'd seen his face after he'd caught me on the stairs during his argument with Captain Croft. I was the last person he wanted anything to do with. I would have to find another way to gather clues.

Just then, a crew member walked by, pulling a massive steamer trunk behind him.

"There are valuables in there. Please be careful. Don't just throw it in with the cargo. Treat it kindly." A woman was trailing behind him, barking orders. She wore a brown, shin-length skirt, a long-sleeved top, and a knitted vest over it, a hand pressed to her felt hat to keep it from blowing away in the wind.

"Yes, ma'am," said the crew member—a middle-aged man with red cheeks and a bald spot. He looked as though he wanted to throw the woman overboard, but instead he just continued nodding, assuring her he would take great care of her belongings.

"If that trunk is lost, I will be in London with absolutely nothing," she said. "Everything I own in the world is in there."

"I understand, ma'am. Everything will be fine. The hold is full of valuables, and we do our best to take special care of them."

The duo disappeared down a flight of stairs that lead below deck, and I shook my head as the woman's droning voice continued to drift up to me. How many different ways could the man have assured her he would keep her belongings safe? It was ridiculous. Hundreds of passengers had their belongings stored below deck to be collected upon their departure, and they weren't hounding the ship's crew about keeping them safe.

Then, an idea struck.

Hundreds of passengers had their belongings stored below deck. Including Colonel Stratton.

I rose to my feet, stretched, and followed the same trail the woman and crew member had just cut across the deck towards the stairs that lead into the belly of the ship.

The passageway was narrow and illuminated by small yellow lights bolted into the ceiling. The lights stretched my shadow halfway down the stairs. I moved steadily downwards for what felt like several minutes before finally reaching the ground. The woman's voice had disappeared by the time I reached the landing, so I had no way of knowing exactly which path they'd taken. A seemingly endless white hallway stretched out on either side of me, and after a few seconds of internal debate, I went to the right. Identical doors dotted the walls, and I jiggled every handle as I passed. Each door was locked. There was no signage anywhere that clearly stated 'crew only,' but the narrow hallway, lack of good lights, and skimpy décor gave me that vibe. Passengers weren't expected to wander these halls.

Suddenly, a door opened further down the hallway. With nowhere to hide, I was entirely exposed, but luckily the crew member—the same one from the deck just a few moments ago—was headed the opposite direction, his back to me. The woman was nowhere in sight. He turned into another corridor, and I quickly moved down the hallway and pushed on the door he'd walked out of. It was unlocked.

The room in front of me was massive. The ceilings were low, eight-feet tall at most, but the space stretched at least half the length of the ship, and was stuffed full of large furniture, cars, stacks of wooden crates and trunks with thick rope netting laying over the top and fastened into hooks in the floor. It was a museum of people's lives. One stack had bundles of canvases leaning against trunks and arranged into precarious towers, oil paintings peeking out from under cotton coverings. Another was crates of wine and liquor, vineyard names stamped on the side in blue ink. It was a quick peek into the lives of the people on board the *RMS Star of India*. I thought of my own belongings, loosely packed into a cheap trunk the Worthings had purchased for me from a shop down the street from the hospital. I hadn't been able to pack any of my things because the authorities thought it was too risky for me to return to the house I'd called home during my stay in India. They weren't yet sure whether the explosion was a planned attack or random, so my survival was being kept quiet until I was safely out of the country. If someone were to peek into my trunk, the only thing they'd learn was that I had far more books than clothes.

As I meandered the rows, enjoying the glimpse into the lives of my fellow passengers, I realized I had no hope of finding the Stratton's storage area. The piles were positioned inside of squares painted on the floor and each square had a number and letter label, but I had no way of knowing which was registered to Colonel Stratton.

"What are you looking for?"

The voice scared me, and I screamed, jumping back and slamming into a car. The sheet covering the vehicle caught on the bracelet around my wrist and slipped to the floor, revealing the shiny burgundy paint color. But I couldn't focus on that. A young Indian boy, no older than twelve, wearing a stained cream tunic and long black pants was peeking out from behind a stack of wooden crates.

"Who are you?" I asked, taking a step towards him and crouching down.

"My name is Aseem," he said in perfect English, a white grin splitting his face. "Are you looking for your luggage?"

I had so many questions for the boy, but still I nodded.

"What's your number?"

I narrowed my eyes at him and he pointed to a spot next to my feet. I followed his finger and saw the "H56" painted on the floor. "Oh, I'm not sure," I said.

"Name?" he asked, his voice all business. I felt as if I'd fallen and hit my head. What was this child doing down with the cargo?

I hesitated. "Stratton."

He raised one dark, feathery eyebrow, and then waved for me to follow him. He moved quickly, his feet silent on the floor, as we wove down the aisles and around cargo. Finally, he stopped and pointed to a modest area along the wall. B36. A navy-blue steamer trunk with gold fixtures was the only item in the space.

"The Colonel had everything but this trunk removed from the space this morning," Aseem said, glancing sideways at me. "I know your name isn't Stratton."

I looked down at the child. His cheeks were flushed and his hair was mussed in the back from sleep. "How long have you been down here?" I asked.

He looked away from me. "Just a little while."

"I don't believe you," I said.

"Then we both have our secrets," he responded, turning back to me. His eyes were wide and dark, and I felt exposed as he studied me. The boy was young, but smart.

"How did you know this space belonged to the Strattons?" I asked.

He shrugged his thin shoulders.

"Have you been hiding down here?"

Suddenly, his cool demeanor vanished. He looked up at

me, eyes wide and panicked. "Please don't tell anyone. I haven't taken anything or done anything wrong. I just wanted to leave Bombay, but I couldn't afford a ticket."

I held out a hand to stop him, and he bit back his words, lips tucked in. "I won't tell anyone you are here."

"Thank you so—"

"If," I said, interrupting him. "You help me."

He tilted his head to the side. "How can I help you?"

"Hiding down here has given you an insight into the ship's passengers that I don't have. Plus, you move quietly, and are clearly adept at gathering information."

Aseem didn't need any more convincing of his talents. He crossed his arms and nodded. "What do you need to know?"

"You said the Colonel had everything removed from this space this morning. How did you know that?"

"A few members of the crew came down this morning and loaded everything up," he said, waving his hand over the nearly empty square. "The blue trunk wouldn't fit on the luggage cart, so they said they'd come back for it. They never did."

The trunk was small and unassuming, and the only access I had to the Strattons private life unless I wanted to break into their cabin.

"Are you going to look inside?" Aseem asked.

"I'm not sure yet," I admitted. It was true. Once I opened the trunk, I would be crossing an invisible line in the sand. I would officially be violating the Stratton's privacy, and throwing myself into the midst of something I didn't yet understand. I'd already come this far, however. It seemed like a waste to walk away without at least taking a peek. "Aseem, would you guard the corridor?"

Aseem's face split in a mischievous smile, and he ran

silently across the floor, his slight body leaning against the wall next to the entrance.

I crossed the painted line on the floor, stepping into the space reserved for the Stratton's belongings. The steamer trunk sat in the center of the space, almost as if it had been staged that way. It didn't seem like an item that had been accidentally left behind. It looked like bait. As I knelt down on the cold floor, my dress fanned out around me, I had to wonder whether I wasn't falling into a trap.

The trunk had a latch, but if there had ever been a lock, it was long gone now. I flipped the latch, dropping it up onto the lid where it clanked with a satisfying metal sound, and then lifted the lid up. The hinges on the back of the trunk squealed as it opened, the sound echoing off the metal walls, making me wince. I knew Aseem and I were likely the only people around—most everyone was enjoying the ship's amenities before lunch—but still, I imagined crew members charging into the cargo hold, hauling me to my feet, and escorting me to Captain Croft. When the room remained silent aside from my labored breathing, I looked down into the trunk.

It appeared to belong to Ruby. Gauzy gowns, long stockings, and a number of different hats were tucked neatly into the bottom. The hats had been settled on top of everything so as not to crush the paper flowers affixed to them. I pulled them out and set them carefully on the floor next to me. Then, I removed the dresses one by one, refolding them into a neat pile. Each one was more elaborate than the next, featuring layers of lace and satin, delicate hemlines, and thick ribbons running around the center.

As I pulled out the last gown, however, it revealed a small label in the back wall of the trunk. It was a square piece of cloth glued to the paper lining. Someone had written on it, but the ink had faded with time. I leaned forward to read it.

Elizabeth Stratton
London, England

ELIZABETH? Could that be Ruby's full name? She wouldn't have been the first woman to shirk the formal moniker in favor of a more unique nickname, that was for sure. The trunk clearly belonged to a woman. Maybe the Colonel had a sister? Or a mother?

"Miss, someone is coming," Aseem hissed. He had come up behind me, though I hadn't heard his footsteps. "I heard talking in the hallway. It's growing closer."

His eyes darted around nervously.

"You can go, Aseem," I said. "Thank you for your help."

He sighed with relief and began backing away towards the maze of cargo. "You know where to find me, miss."

I glanced back at the door, and by the time I turned around, Aseem was gone. It seemed as though he would be more useful than I had initially thought.

Mindful of his warning, I grabbed a pile of the dresses from the floor next to me and dropped them into the steamer trunk. As they landed in the bottom in a tangle of fabric and ribbons, I noticed the corner of the trunk lining peeling up. I quickly reached in to smooth it down, but when I pushed on it, the whole bottom of the trunk shifted. Knowing I was short on time, but unable to walk away from the puzzle before me, I hurriedly wedged my fingers between the cardboard trunk bottom and the wall of the trunk and pulled up.

It lifted out easily to reveal a second compartment below the main one. The trunk had a false bottom, but why? Since I couldn't yet hear the approaching voices or footsteps, I estimated I had maybe another minute left. I pulled the bottom out, dumping the dresses once again on the floor next to me.

A stack of folded letters sat in one corner. I opened one, and scanned over it quickly, looking for any details that jumped out. The letter was addressed to Ruby and signed, "Love Always, Mo Mo."

A secret affair, perhaps? Ruby was young and had a taste for handsome men, so it wouldn't be too far-fetched to believe her capable of such a thing. However, the letter merely discussed the rainy weather in London and a new coat the writer had bought for winter. And the handwriting, although careless and uneven, looked distinctly feminine. The letters were looped and curled in a way few men would take the time to do. Also, the paper was the palest shade of pink. However, I could glean little else from the contents.

Now I heard them. The sound of the approaching voices Aseem had warned me of. They sounded near enough that I knew I was almost out of time.

I glanced hastily at the rest of the letters, but nothing stood out to my eyes. Ruby had been involved in a correspondence she wished to keep secret, but I did not know with whom, aside from the nickname "Mo Mo."

Other than the letters, the trunk contained a small silver locket engraved with the letter 'M' and a single photograph. The voices in the corridor were just outside the door, so I had but seconds to look at the image. The picture showed a young girl—blonde and no older than seven—sitting in a white wicker chair against a black backdrop. Her cheeks were flushed, and her hair fell in ringlets around her cherubic face. She had wide eyes that seemed to stare into mine, and I found myself captivated by her. Could she be "Mo Mo?"

"Where is Stratton's space?" a voice asked.

"I'll have to check the ledger," a second voice answered. "Howard said he emptied the space this morning, but the Colonel insists he is missing a piece of luggage."

I hadn't heard the door to the cargo hold open, but the voices were echoing around the room, and by the sound of it, they would be standing before me in only a few minutes. As quickly and quietly as possible, I replaced the letters and the photograph in the bottom of the trunk, repositioned the false bottom, and stacked the dresses in as nice a pile as time would allow. I lowered the lid, letting it thud softly closed.

"The Strattons are in space B36," the second voice said. "Shocking about the wife. Do you think the husband capable of murder?"

The men were nearly upon me, and I knew I needed to get out fast. I couldn't cut across the aisle lest they see me. My only option was to hide in one of the nearby spaces and hope they wouldn't look too closely. If only I had Aseem's penchant for quiet movement and finding clever hiding spots.

I ducked across the gap between the Strattons' space and B37, which had a large collection of marble busts and sculptures filling the small square, and ducked behind a rather muddy depiction of King George V.

"The Colonel seems hot-tempered enough to kill. His wife was murdered last night, but he still found twenty minutes to scream at Howard in the hallway. That missing trunk must be full of gold," the man said.

Or full of secrets, I thought. The trunk didn't seem as if it would be of much importance to Colonel Stratton, being filled with dresses and hats, but perhaps the bottom compartment wasn't as secret as it seemed. The letters had been addressed to Ruby, but that didn't mean she had received them. Perhaps the Colonel was keeping them from her, but why? And who was the girl in the photo?

The men rounded the corner, both wearing white uniforms and matching caps. They pulled a luggage cart behind them.

One of the men—tall with a mop of blonde hair hanging across his forehead—bent down and picked up the trunk. "It's definitely not full of gold. It barely weights ten pounds."

He dropped it onto the cart with a thud, giving little concern for the safety of the contents.

"Then I suppose it will actually make it to his room," the other man said. "If it had been full of gold, I may have told the Colonel we couldn't find it."

I suddenly wondered whether Lady Dixon's brooch hadn't been stolen after all. If all the crew were as trustworthy as the two men currently rolling the steamer trunk away, I was going to have to keep an eye on my own belongings.

The men left, but I stayed hidden for several more minutes out of an abundance of caution. I wished I'd kept even one of the letters as evidence. Of what, I wasn't sure, but the hidden compartment felt important. People didn't make a habit of hiding things of no import. When I finally came out of my hiding place and moved towards the door, I called out for Aseem, but my voice echoed off the walls without response.

7

Mr. and Mrs. Worthing spent the second half of the afternoon and half of dinner talking about how invigorating they had found their game of badminton.

"Our partners were less than adequate at the sport, but the exercise felt invigorating," Mr. Worthing said, talking to a half-full table that had fully grown weary of the subject.

I did my best to smile and nod, but even my thoughts began to wander as the discussion drug on and on. It didn't help that in addition to the starting absence of Ruby Stratton, we were also missing the company of Colonel Stratton and Dr. Rushforth. Colonel Stratton's absence made sense—his wife had just died. It would have raised more than a few eyebrows if he had appeared at dinner as though nothing had happened. Dr. Rushforth's absence was unexplained, but not altogether worthy of note. There was no assigned seating, and as I'd witnessed only that morning, he enjoyed eating at the veranda café on occasion.

"Yes, the other couple won't be going professional anytime soon"—Mrs. Worthing paused to laugh at the criticism—"but it is amazing to be able to play a full game of badminton on a ship. Can you believe it? We played badminton while floating in the Arabian Sea?"

"Truly a marvel of human invention," Mr. Worthing added.

"No sign of my brooch," Lady Dixon interjected with a sigh. "I fear it is gone for good."

Between the Worthings and Lady Dixon, I feared the evening's conversation would be far from enjoyable. Lady Dixon had been huffing and sighing all morning at the loss of her brooch, simultaneously certain she would never find it, but also unwilling to give up the search.

"Do not say that," her niece Jane said quietly. "I'm sure we will find it yet."

Lady Dixon scowled at her niece and shook her head. "Your childlike naiveté is growing tiresome, Jane. It is not lost. It was stolen."

The young girl flinched at the woman's harsh words and cast her gaze down into her soup. The night before, Jane had helped herself to a large portion of bread, and Lady Dixon had warned her against eating too much and losing her womanly shape. Since then, the girl had stuck to soups and fruit, and I would have sworn her cheekbones had grown sharper, even though it had only been twenty-four hours.

"You'd be surprised how things thought gone can turn up," I said, offering Jane a conspiratorial smile which she didn't return. She had seemed friendly enough to me the first time we'd met but her aunt's poor opinion of me must have been contagious.

Lady Dixon didn't even bother looking at me. She simply sighed louder and shook her head again. "I'd hoped this ship would be peopled with enough high society to prevent these kinds of crimes, but in this day and age, there is no safe place. They like to call theft a petty crime, but there is nothing petty about breaking the law. If you want my true feelings on the issue, all criminals should be put to death. It's the only way to ensure criminals do not breed more criminals."

"Do you ever offer anything but your true feelings on any subject, Lady Dixon?" I asked. The woman gave her rather severe opinion openly and without shame. I didn't think her capable of a half-truth or a white lie. She had no desire to spare anyone's feelings but her own.

"We won the badminton game, though, of course, I felt it impolite to keep an official score," Mrs. Worthing cut in, continuing her own topic. She seemed to pay little mind to Lady Dixon, who, if eyes could kill, would have murdered me several times over. "We played for fun, after all."

"I do not waste my time with half-truths," Lady Dixon said, eyes focused somewhere over my head. "My opinions may be harsh, but I believe more people should learn to accept criticism aimed at their betterment. Take Jane, for instance. When her mother sent her to live with me, she was wild. Now, after six months in my home, she is half-wild, which is a marked improvement."

Jane's cheeks reddened considerably, but she smiled up at her aunt and nodded her head in agreement.

Mrs. Worthing spooned out a scoop of green beans and hovered the spoon in front of her mouth. "Perhaps, Mr. Worthing, we will be able to convince our Rose to join us in the court tomorrow," Mrs. Worthing said.

Mr. Worthing's eyes brightened at the idea. "What a marvelous plan, dear."

It would be rude to explain to them how little I desired to spend the day on a badminton court with the two of them, especially in the midst of Ruby Stratton's murder investigation, so I scrambled for another excuse.

"I wouldn't have a partner," I said with a shrug. "It would hardly be fair to play two-on-one."

"Perhaps, Jane could assist with—"

"No." Lady Dixon barked, cutting Mrs. Worthing off.

For the first time, Mrs. Worthing seemed to acknowledge Lady Dixon. She looked from the old woman to me and back again, trying to sort out when exactly the conversation had veered away from her own story.

Jane sipped her soup, and only chanced a glance in Lady Dixon's direction when she was certain the old woman had stopped glaring at her. I wondered whether Jane had always been a nervous creature, or whether endless months of Lady Dixon's instruction had sucked the willpower from her.

"We met a nice couple down at the courts this morning," Mr. Worthing said. "They would almost certainly be up for a match. We don't need to force the young ladies to spend any more time with the old folk than they already do."

Mrs. Worthing took great offense to Mr. Worthing's description of her, but she expressed it by remaining resolutely silent the remainder of the dinner, even when her husband spoke to her directly. Lady Dixon made mention of her brooch several more times, but similar to badminton, the table had been saturated with the topic all day and had nothing more to say on the subject. I used the uncomfortable silence to think through what my next step in the investigation should be.

I wanted to find a reason to implicate Lady Dixon in the crime. In addition to knowing Ruby prior to boarding the *RMS Star of India*, she also had an impossible moral standard by which anyone and everyone was judged. Ruby had far from met this standard, and Lady Dixon had said herself only a few minutes before that she believed all criminals should be put to death. Could Ruby's flirtation with the Captain, among other men—verging on adultery in Lady Dixon's mind—have been reason enough for her to harm the young woman? It was a possibility I had to consider, mostly because imprisonment would be the only thing that could lower Lady Dixon's opinion of herself.

Overhearing Colonel Stratton's conversation with the Captain had certainly piqued my interest, and the secret compartment in the trunk hadn't provided anything immediately incriminating, but the secret compartment was certainly a point of interest. Aside from entering the Colonel's room—which I had no reason to believe he would be vacating anytime soon—I had no other access point to the inner workings of his life. All of the cargo stored below deck had been rolled up to the stateroom Colonel Stratton and Ruby had, only the day before, shared. I needed to find someone who could give me a glimpse into his personality. I had gathered very little from the previous evening at dinner.

Suddenly, I recalled the one detail the Colonel had mentioned the previous night. As everyone had stood to leave the table, he'd informed Ruby he would be going to the smoking lounge.

"On the first night?" she had asked, glancing around the table and then settling her eyes on her husband. It was clear she wished he would accompany her back to the room instead.

He nodded and smiled, addressing the table. "Might as well establish my routine early. I intend to join the men there every evening."

Dr. Rushforth had voiced his intent to take a brandy there before heading to bed, but Mr. Worthing promised the

Colonel he would accompany him there the next evening. The day had been too exciting, and he was ready for bed.

"Is it only for men?" Ruby asked, wrapping a hand around her husband's elbow.

He extricated himself and pushed his chair into the table. "As an unspoken rule, yes. Don't worry, I will join you in the room once the smoke and brandy run out."

As he left, he had whispered loudly to Dr. Rushforth that the ship had three weeks' worth of liquor and smokes. "It won't run out until dawn."

8

The lounge was wood-paneled, and I viewed it through a thick haze of smoke. Men in white shirts and loose ties, jackets draped over the backs of their chairs filled the room. Black-toed oxfords kicked up on the tables, as if their wearers had no worries of scuffing the freshly lacquered wood. The room's occupants threw their heads back and laughed, mouths open, the sound filling the room as much as the smoke.

It took me a moment to realize that I, a woman, was entering the sacred space of men. I had been standing in the doorway for a spell, and the men had begun to take notice. As I looked around the room again, it had grown considerably less raucous, and I was drawing attention.

Walking into the room had felt like a good idea before I'd actually done it. If anyone on the ship had heard Colonel Stratton's true feelings, it would have been one of the men in the smoking lounge. As I stood there, though, I wanted nothing more than to leave. Instead, I walked into the room with a purpose, hoping my confidence would stave off any men who felt the need to inform me I was not allowed in their space.

I didn't immediately recognize anyone in the room, so I headed for the back corner where a fully stocked bar cart sat. The bottles were all various shapes and sizes of glass, and annoyingly unlabeled. I had very little experience with liquors, so I was trying to convince myself to reach for a bottle, pour myself a glass, and face whatever consequences arose, when a man strolled up next to me.

"Would you like me to make you a drink?" he asked, reaching for a glass before I could even answer.

"Do I look incapable?" I asked haughtily, though I was silently thanking the heavens for his arrival.

He raised an eyebrow at me and then laughed. "I hope my offer was not misconstrued. Any woman willing to walk in here alone is clearly capable of anything. I simply hoped to start a conversation."

"Then you've succeeded," I said, leaning toward him slightly.

He poured a finger's worth of some brown liquor into my glass, and I sipped it in such microscopic amounts that I felt only the slightest sting as it dripped down my throat.

"Are you here for the full journey, or do you plan to stop off at one of the ports?" the man asked.

"I'm headed to London. And you?"

He smiled and rolled up the sleeves of his white shirt to the elbow. His suspenders were bright red, the same shade as his hair. "Perhaps I will see you in London sometime, then?"

I pressed a hand to my chest. "You can't possibly expect me to set up a date with someone who hasn't even given me their full name, can you?"

He shook his head, his cheeks flaming. Very rarely had I

encountered a man with enough humility to blush out of embarrassment. "Thomas Arbuckle."

I extended my hand to him, bent daintily at the wrist. "Rose Beckingham."

He squeezed my hand and bent low to kiss my fingers. Suddenly, I was the one blushing. Thomas Arbuckle was a multi-faceted man, and he almost made me forget my purpose for entering the lounge. Almost.

"Are you in the lounge often?" I asked.

He hesitated. "I don't wish for my answer to upset you," he admitted. "If I say yes, you may think me a lazy drunk. If I say no, you may find me to be boring. Which answer would please you most?"

"The truth," I said plainly.

"It's the second night on the ship, and my second night in the lounge," he said, head hanging down. "However, if you find that unappealing, I'll never set foot in here again."

I smoothed down my midnight blue satin gown, and readjusted my sequined headband in my hair, moving a golden curl from over my eye. "That won't be necessary, Thomas. Your frequency here could actually be of some use to me."

"Then, I will spend every moment of the next three weeks here," he gushed, grabbing my hand with both of his and leading me to a recently vacated table against the wall. "Anything you need."

I laughed, unable to hide my amusement at his eagerness. "That is a dangerous offer, Mr. Arbuckle. You know little of me as a person. What if I need something truly nefarious?"

He shook his head vehemently. "Forgive me, Ma'am, but no one with a face so angelic could be evil."

I tossed my head back and laughed, reminding myself of

the men I'd observed upon first entering the lounge. The atmosphere apparently lent itself to full-bodied laughter. "Lucky for you, I need nothing more than your recollection. Do you recall seeing a square-shaped man, past military, bright red face—?"

Thomas interrupted my question with a groan. "Yet another woman ensnared by a military man? I never would have thought I'd regret not spending time on the battlefield."

"You have it all wrong. I have no interest in this man. Not romantically, at least." I lowered my voice and leaned forward. "His wife was murdered early this morning."

"Oh, you mean the Colonel?" Thomas asked at normal volume, drawing the attention of a few men around us.

"I do have another request," I said as gently as possible. "I don't want it widely known that I'm asking about the Colonel."

He pressed a hand to his mouth and nodded in understanding. "What would you like to know?"

"I have reason to believe he was here last night?"

"Yes, most of the evening, in fact," Thomas said, nodding. Then, his neck shrunk down into his shoulders. "I have just revealed that I was here most of the evening, as well. Please assure me that is not an issue."

Thomas intrigued me, but I did not think I would be able to spend any considerable amount of time with a man who needed such constant reassurance.

I ignored his request and moved forward with my questioning. "Did he do or say anything that caused any concern or brought you pause?"

Thomas rolled his eyes upward, as if trying to peer into his own thoughts, and then shook his head. "I don't remember anything sticking out. He certainly dominated the room, though. Every man here was crowded around his table. He mostly spoke of his time in the war. Why do you ask?"

I'd thought it obvious, but apparently, I would have to explain it fully to Thomas. "The man's wife was murdered," I reminded him, pausing to see if Thomas's expression would change from one of mild puzzlement to understanding. When it didn't, I continued. "I'm curious whether or not he could have done it."

Thomas reared back as if I'd slapped him. "The Colonel? A murderer?" He shook his head. "Impossible."

"Not impossible, exactly," I said. "He spent many years in the war. Men in war do an awful lot of killing."

"That is different," he said, though he offered no explanation for how exactly it was different. "I spent the evening with him. Even the thought that he could have left here and then murdered his wife hours later is too dark to consider. I can't dwell on it a moment longer."

Thomas Arbuckle truly looked as though he could swoon, and I wondered whether the smoking lounge didn't make a habit of allowing women in, after all. The thought felt too harsh a criticism on the many women I did know who wouldn't even bat an eye at the idea of the Colonel murdering Ruby Stratton. Thomas Arbuckle had the constitution of a plucked tulip in the summer heat—he threatened to wilt at the slightest upset.

"I do not wish to distress you, but do you think you could tell me when exactly the Colonel left for the evening?" I asked.

Thomas shook his head, considerably less eager to assist me. "In fact, I can. I assisted him back to his room."

"Assisted him?"

"The Colonel had a bit too much to drink. He is a solid

man, so I would not say he was drunk, but he stumbled several times on his way out, and I chose to see him safely to his room. A ship is no place to be unsteady on your feet. The last thing I wanted was for the man to go overboard."

"That is very kind of you. So, when exactly did you see him to his room?" I asked.

"It was just before three AM," Thomas said. "He looked tired and said he would go to bed immediately."

It was apparent Mr. Arbuckle was trying to persuade me to believe the Colonel impossible of the murder.

"When you delivered the Colonel to his room, did you happen to see his wife?" I asked.

Thomas cast his eyes to the side, but I could tell he was in deep thought. Then, he looked to me, eyes clear, and shook his head. "I did not. The Colonel used his key to open the door, and the room was dark. I assumed the lady to be asleep, but I can't say for sure. I now believe she had left the room the night before, perhaps in search of her husband, when she met her fate. The Colonel could not have had anything to do with it."

I knew for a fact the Colonel went straight from dinner to the lounge and, according to Thomas Arbuckle, he went straight from the lounge to his cabin. Thomas had opinions about Mrs. Stratton's whereabouts, but I knew nothing of her movements the night before her death. I did have a clearer picture of the Colonel's, though. If the Colonel had been responsible for killing his wife, it would have had to have been between the hours of three and seven in the morning because I had seen him in the hallway in the morning when the crew member came to deliver the news of the murder.

"I know the thought is a dark one, especially since you were with Colonel Stratton that morning, but from what you learned of him last night, do you believe him to be a man capable of murder?" I asked, though I felt certain I already knew the answer.

Thomas shook his head, picked up his drink, and rose to his feet, prepared to leave me, despite promising only minutes before that he would spend the entirety of the ship's voyage in the room if I asked. "I do not. He seemed a good, brave man. He told stories of other men he'd met in the war—terrible men with dark pasts. Whatever man killed Mrs. Stratton is certainly more like those other men, monsters who will be revealed in due time."

"You are certain her killer is a man?"

"Of course it was a man. A woman would not have the stomach for such a crime," he said.

Thomas had a simple view of the world. One in which monsters, rather than hiding amongst us, blending in and deceiving us, made themselves apparent. One in which men were strong, and women were sensitive, in need of protecting. I felt it was good he had not endured the war, as I was almost positive he would not have survived it.

"I'm sure you're right. Thank you for your help."

Thomas wished me luck in discovering whatever I was searching for, though he said it with little conviction, and then moved deeper into the hazy room, blending in with the rest of the men's faces. I waited a few moments to see if another man would approach me, but none did. So, I swallowed the remainder of my drink, wincing as it burned down my throat and settled in my stomach, and left.

Mrs. Worthing knocked on my door before going to bed and insisted on laying her eyes on me before her mind could be settled.

"Promise me you will stay in your room, Rose," she said,

eyes wide and desperate. "I couldn't bear it if anything happened to you."

I grabbed her hands in mine. Although Mrs. Worthing was certainly a silly woman, her heart had made more than enough room for me, and I was grateful. "I have no reason to leave, I assure you. I will meet you in the sitting room for breakfast?"

"Yes, please," she said. "Crepes are on the program for tomorrow."

I lay in bed for a while before falling asleep, staring up at the low ceiling of my cabin. In the light of day, surrounded by the other passengers, the idea of the Colonel murdering his wife didn't seem too far-fetched, and it didn't create any amount of unease inside of me. Lying alone in my room, however, with the Colonel living one wall away from me, I couldn't help but feel unsettled. If he was the murderer, had he done it in their cabin? Had it happened only a few feet away while I slept in my bed, blissfully unaware of the horror Ruby Stratton was facing?

The image of Ruby Stratton looking into my face when I found her in the ladies room, eyes large and fearful as she told me she was afraid for her life, filled my mind as I drifted into a restless sleep.

9

Though Mrs. Worthing had asked me not to leave my cabin before I fell asleep, I somehow found myself in the hallway. The overhead lights flickered and then burnt out, casting the corridor in inky shadows that crept up the walls and swallowed the red glare of the emergency lights so I couldn't even see my own feet on the floor. As blackness surrounded me, I began to feel the rush of cold water against my ankles. But still, I continued to move forward. Towards what, I didn't know. I only knew I didn't want to stand still. With every step, the water rose higher. It washed over my calves, my knees, my thighs until my dress fanned out around me on the surface of the water. The icy waves bit at my skin, sprouting goosebumps down my arms and legs. Was the ship sinking? Had we struck something? It certainly wouldn't be the first time a large ship had sunk, but Mr. Worthing had assured me and his wife both that the *RMS Star of India* was the best engineered passenger ship on the ocean, and it would be nearly impossible for us to sink.

The blackness began to dissipate, though the water was

still pouring in at an ever-increasing rate, and faceless people began filing out of their cabins and trudging through the water next to me. I tried to stop them, ask what was happening, but no one seemed to be able to hear me. I reached out to stop a woman moving down the hallway holding the hand of a small child, but my hand moved straight through her as though she were an apparition. I screamed, and still no one budged.

Then, I heard the yelling. I spun in a quick circle, wondering whether someone hadn't heard me and was trying to respond. But then I realized the screaming was muddled, coming from a room off the hallway. It was the same fighting I'd heard my first day on the ship. I turned to my left, and despite having walked for several minutes, I found myself outside the Stratton's cabin, less than three feet from my own cabin door. The yelling grew louder.

"Help me!" I heard Ruby's voice, desperate and hoarse, begging for help. I hadn't been able to hear what she'd been saying the first day, but now the words felt as though they were echoing in my own head.

I took a step forward and tried to bang on the door, but it wouldn't make a sound. I screamed and flailed my arms, but my fists remained silent against the metal.

I could hear Ruby struggling for breath, could practically feel her life slipping away, but no matter how hard I tried, I couldn't do anything to help her.

"I'm sorry, Ruby," I began to scream, hot tears streaming down my face, as salty as the ocean water running through the hallway. "I'm so sorry."

Then, everything froze. The water grew still and stagnant, the flashing emergency lights stilled, emitting a constant red hue, casting the hallway in a blood red. I reached for the Strattons' door knob, and my fingers connected with the cool metal. With a trembling hand I turned the knob and pushed the door open.

The room was stacked high with boxes and cargo, everything from the storage space below deck. I called out for Ruby, but no one answered. Hesitantly, I tried for Colonel Stratton, as well, but still, nothing.

Then, I noticed the blue steamer trunk sitting on the bed. The latch had been flipped open, but the trunk was still closed. I wanted to see the photograph of the young girl again. I wanted to read more of the correspondence between Ruby and Mo Mo. I wanted to know what their relationship was, what they talked about. Had Ruby mentioned any marital problems to Mo Mo? Or, had Ruby known about the letters at all? It was possible the Colonel had been keeping them from her. I had to open the trunk again and see if I'd missed anything the first time.

I reached out for the trunk, and as my hand connected with the sides where it was edged in polished brass, I saw a single red drop run out from under the lid. It splattered on the white bed spread, but it was too late to stop. I was already lifting the lid. I dropped it and it clattered open. A scream stuck in my throat. The lid fell back with a thud, jolting the trunk and sending it tumbling to the floor. It tipped over, and Ruby's lifeless body fell at my feet.

I woke up in a cold sweat, my nightgown drenched and clinging to me. The clock on the mantle said it was only four in the morning, but I knew I wouldn't be able to fall back asleep. The nightmare had been horrible, and I hadn't thought anything could be worse than the dreams I'd had about the explosion in Simla. Whenever I'd closed my eyes in the weeks since the tragedy, I'd seen smoke and blood splatter, the corpse-like hand of my dear friend. Now, I was seeing Ruby Stratton.

Even in my mind, though, no killer emerged. I didn't see a hint of the murderer or any clues I'd missed in my waking hours that had become clear in my subconscious. It was just the horror of her death.

Despite the dream, I touched up the finger curls in my hair, slipped into a purple tea dress—matching fringe hanging from the hem and the loose sleeves—and left the claustrophobic space of the cabin. I wrote a note for Mrs. Worthing and left it on the sitting room sofa, informing her I had not been murdered, but had, rather, gone on an early morning walk to let the sea air clear my head. I told her I wouldn't be back until mid-morning. Hopefully the letter would stop her worrying.

As I moved through the ship, the dream clung to me like a fog. I knew it had been nothing but the imaginings of my overworked mind, but still, the image of Ruby Stratton's beautiful face cold and pale in front of me resurfaced with each blink. And more, I wanted to know who had killed her. I wanted to know who had caused her such pain.

Thomas Arbuckle didn't believe Colonel Stratton capable of murder, but I couldn't yet rule out a single suspect. Far and away, the Colonel seemed like the most likely suspect. His behavior after his wife's murder had not seemed to be the actions of a man deep in the throes of grief. Rather, he seemed guilty, lurking around the edges of rooms, taking all of his luggage from the cargo hold into his cabin, and trying to make a profit by blackmailing Captain Croft. But odd behavior alone was not a sure sign of guilt. I needed more evidence.

I was dimly aware in the back of my mind that my

growing obsession with Ruby's death was probably a reaction to my own recent trauma. The explosion had happened and I had run away from India. Now, I couldn't run away from my thoughts and so I sought to distract them by focusing on someone else's tragedy. Even knowing all of this, I couldn't resist sinking deeper into the mystery of Ruby's murder.

The ship was almost entirely deserted so early in the morning, save for a few crew members. I wandered the deck until the dark of night gave way to an orange and pink sunrise over the ocean. I made loop after loop, running my mind over the facts and the suspects, trying to see anything I'd missed. Finally, as passengers began to emerge from below deck, eyes still swollen with sleep, I hatched a plan.

Although I had six suspects, one of them—Colonel Stratton—had made himself more obvious a suspect than the others. So, it only made sense for me to focus on him until I could either prove he had committed the murder or rule him out as a suspect. My first order of business, I decided, would be to speak with Captain Croft. Not only could he give me more information about Ruby's death—considering he knew nearly everything that happened on the ship—but he had also been accused of the murder by Colonel Stratton. If anyone had a deeper insight into the Colonel's thought process, it would have to be the Captain.

I decided I would see the Captain right away, before breakfast, even. However, that plan was quickly spoiled by the arrival of Mr. and Mrs. Worthing.

"There you are, Rose," Mrs. Worthing gushed, coming up behind me and wrapping me in a tight hug. "I was worried sick about you."

"Didn't you find my note?" I asked, pulling myself from her arms and smoothing down my dress.

"I saw it, but didn't feel confident you had written it," she said, eyes wide and watery. "What if the killer had written the note on your behalf to buy himself more time? You really shouldn't leave the cabin so early. Nothing happens on deck before breakfast, so there truly isn't any need."

"I couldn't sleep," I said.

Mrs. Worthing decided that portion of the conversation was over, and transitioned from lecturing me into offering a broad smile, her hands pressed together excitedly. "We have the best news," she said.

I raised my eyebrows, expectant. Mrs. Worthing nudged her husband, and he jolted as though he had fallen asleep standing up. He looked from his wife to me, and then seemed to remember something. "Oh yes, the absolute best news."

"We spoke with the couple we played badminton with yesterday," Mrs. Worthing said, pausing for dramatic effect. "And they said they would love to have a third team member."

That was the amazing news they'd been waiting to tell me. Typically, I would have pretended to be as ecstatic as they were, but it was early, I hadn't slept well, and confusion kept me neutral. "Isn't badminton typically played in teams of one or two?" I asked.

"Yes, obviously," Mrs. Worthing said, annoyed that I hadn't seemed to catch her meaning straight away. "But they've agreed to rotate you in and out of the game between matches. We beat them so handily yesterday, I'm sure they are anxious to redeem themselves, and having you play with them is their only shot."

"I don't believe I'm even familiar with the rules of badminton," I said, desperate for a way to avoid spending the day below deck with the Worthings. Guilt crept into my stomach. They were kind people who clearly only wanted the best for me, but I also found them to be the two silliest people I'd ever met. Too many hours spent with them each day, and I'd find myself going loony.

Mrs. Worthing tilted her head to the side, eyes narrowed. "Your parents always speak highly of your ability on the court," she said, and then her eyes widened. Occasionally, the Worthings forgot about the accident, and would mention my parents in the present tense, and then catch themselves and feel incredibly uncomfortable.

"Of course, well..." I stuttered, fingers playing nervously with the hem of my dress. "I only meant it has been such a long time. I've probably forgotten the rules."

"Nonsense, dear girl," Mr. Worthing said, patting me on the shoulder. "You'll be great. We can assist you if you forget any of the rules. Besides, we are only playing for fun."

"Yes, exactly," Mrs. Worthing agreed, eager to move past her mistake, her cheeks red with embarrassment.

I would have believed them, except for the numerous times they had explained how badly they had beaten their opponents. Still, it didn't seem to matter. The Worthings would not take no for an answer. Immediately after breakfast, I found myself descending the stairs to the racket court.

I hadn't thought to purchase any recreational clothing prior to boarding the ship, so Mrs. Worthing insisted I wear something of hers, despite my rather adamant protests. I walked onto the court sporting a pleated plaid skirt that hung past my knees, a white shirt with collars that flared to the tips of my shoulders, and a loose sweater with a 'W' embroidered over the heart.

"The 'W' stands for Worthing," Mrs. Worthing said as she slipped into a matching sweater in a dark shade of blue.

Walking down the corridor together was mortifying.

The embarrassment only grew worse when we reached the court and I saw Mr. Worthing had a 'W' sweater of his own.

"We look smashing," he said, winking at me.

I did my best to muster up a smile, but luckily, I was spared a response by the arrival of the couple from across the hall. My mouth fell open when I saw them approaching.

"Good morning, Madame," Achilles Prideaux said in his French accent, bending low and kissing Mrs. Worthing's hand.

A curly-haired woman stood next to him, dark and sultry. Her exercise attire was a pleated cream skirt that grazed her knees and a matching shirt that clung temptingly on her curves. I could only imagine the way Lady Dixon would have reacted to her arrival.

"Lena," Mr. Worthing said, embracing the woman and kissing both of her cheeks. She returned the gesture, and I noticed Mrs. Worthing tighten her lips ever so slightly before greeting the woman herself. Mr. Worthing turned away from Lena long enough to point to me standing behind Mrs. Worthing in a desperate attempt to hide my sweater. "Have you met our friend, Rose Beckingham?"

"I have not had the pleasure," Lena said, her accent melodic and alluring. She came towards me, arms extended, and I had no option but to move into her arms and return the hug. She smelled like begonias and vanilla.

I stepped away, and finally looked up at Achilles Prideaux. His skin looked even more tan under the artificial lighting, and his thin mustache was bent around his sly smile. He sported a loose pair of brown pants, cuffed at the ankle and worn high on his waist, with tan suspenders. His button-down shirt was the same shade as Lena's.

"I was lucky enough to cross Mademoiselle Beckingham's path the first night aboard the ship," Achilles said, his voice oil-slick.

"How wonderful," Mrs. Worthing said. "We are already friends, then."

"Friends, indeed," I agreed, looking at Mr. Prideaux.

"Then, let's play!" Mr. Worthing said, handing me a racket. He turned to the Prideauxs "Are you both fine to alternate with Rose?"

"Of course," Lena cried, throwing her arm around my shoulder and leading me to their side of the court. "We are in need of any help we can find."

As it turned out, I was more of a hindrance than anything else. Mrs. Worthing had a deceptively powerful serve, and though she insisted it was luck, she sent the shuttlecock to my side of the court every time.

"So close," Mr. Worthing shouted over to me after I had, once again, swung and missed.

I smiled at him, doing a terrible job at hiding what a horrid time I was having.

"I think you're getting better," Lena said. Really, Lena and Achilles were fine athletes. Bizarrely, if they had been playing anyone other than the Worthings— it was still hard for me to grasp that the couple, who only that morning had spent half an hour discussing the absurdly tall height of the grand staircase in the dining room, were also secret badminton champions—they would have won several matches. But between Mr. and Mrs. Worthing being exceptionally good and me being exceptionally bad, the deck had been stacked against them.

"I'm feeling a bit tired," I said, mostly as an excuse to get off the court for a spell. It was also a little true, though. "I think I'll take a break."

Lena voiced her disappointment, but she also winked at

Achilles, who had been standing on the sidelines, eyeing me while I struggled. I moved in that direction and handed him the racket.

"Sports are not your pastime of choice, I take it?" It felt as though his words were meant to be an insult, but his accent made it difficult to tell the difference.

"Clearly," I said, puckering my mouth and spinning around to face the court, looking past him.

"You do not like me," he said with a smile.

I was taken aback by his boldness. "I do not know you, Monsieur."

"That can be rectified."

Why did Achilles Prideaux make me feel so inadequate? Normally, my quick wit and sharp tongue carried me far, but around him I felt out of my depth. His words my first night on the ship had stuck with me, and I feared what he may know. I took a deep breath, and looked at him, taking in his rich brown eyes and sharply cut cheek bones. Again, I realized how handsome he would be, if only he would shave his thin mustache.

"I'm sure your wife would rather we didn't become too close."

"My wife?" His forehead wrinkled, and for the first time since I'd met him, he looked uncertain. Then, understanding flooded his face. He looked back at Lena who was talking animatedly with the Worthings. "Lena is my sister."

Some detective I was. I hadn't even been able to detect that the Prideauxs were siblings, which now that Achilles informed me of the fact, became obvious. Same olive skin tone, same almond-shaped eyes, same thick black hair— Lena's was wavy, but I suspected Achilles' would be, as well, if he didn't use so much product to slick it back.

"Still," I said, lifting my head, trying to preserve some

dignity. "I don't think it is a good idea for us to become too close."

He turned to wave at Lena, telling her he would be on the court in a minute, and turned back to me. "Would you at least stay behind after this match to speak with me for a moment?"

His eyes were earnest and probing, and though I didn't want to stay behind, and I truly had no intention of doing so, I found myself nodding my consent.

"Thank you," he whispered with a smile, his teeth straight and gleaming.

When he left, a shiver ran through me. I had never met someone capable of throwing me off kilter so easily. He didn't know me, yet he looked at me as though he could read my every thought. And as absurd as the idea sounded, occasionally I felt as though he actually could.

As I stood on the sidelines, watching as the Worthings grew closer to securing yet another victory—though, of course, we weren't really keeping score—a pit began to open up in my stomach. Achilles Prideaux had spoken only a few words to me the first night on the ship, yet they had lingered with me for days. Did I really want to give him that kind of power over me willingly? While the Worthings and the Prideauxs were involved in a rather serious and unusual volley back and forth, I slipped from the court and ran up the stairs two at a time. If Monsieur Prideaux wanted to speak with me, he would have to hunt me down himself.

My fear, though, was that he would do just that.

10

I'd begun the day with high expectations, but the badminton game had exhausted me, and the unexpected run in with the mysterious Achilles Prideaux had me confined to my room through lunch and the majority of the afternoon.

"You left so suddenly," Mrs. Worthing said for the third time. She was standing in the doorway of my cabin, hand on her hip. She had dressed for dinner in a floor-length satin dress the color of peaches. It matched her skin tone beautifully, and she looked at least ten years younger when standing in dim lighting.

"I'm sorry. I wasn't feeling well, but I didn't want to interrupt the game."

"Monsieur Prideaux certainly was sad to see you leave. I think he has taken a fancy to you," she said with a wink.

I tried to fully express not only my repulsion at the idea, but how little stock I placed in it, but Mrs. Worthing insisted on repeating the notion to Mr. Worthing and myself several times on the walk to dinner alone.

Dr. Rushforth joined us once again for dinner, making

no mention of his absence the day before. He sat in the seat next to me, which Lady Dixon didn't seem to approve of.

"How have you been, Rose?" he asked, cutting into his Shepherd's Pie with a fork and knife.

"Very well. And yourself, Dr. Rushforth?" I smiled as I spoke, though I couldn't say exactly why.

"Very *very* well," he said, placing a special amount of emphasis on the second "very."

"That's twice as good as I have been, so congratulations." I could feel Mrs. Worthing eyeing me, wondering when I'd had time to grow so close to Dr. Rushforth, and I was grateful she remained silent. The last thing I needed was her raving on about the number of men showing me special attention in such a short amount of time. I would absolutely die on the spot if she mentioned anything about Achilles Prideaux in front of Dr. Rushforth.

He leaned in to me. "Ruby Stratton still seems to be a large topic of conversation," he whispered, making reference to the wager we'd made. It still felt improper to bet on when everyone would forget about Ruby's murder and move on to more positive conversation topics, but it also gave me a slight rush to have a shared secret with a man as intelligent and powerful as Dr. Rushforth.

I turned my mouth to him, keeping my eyes down on my dinner plate. "It seems as though victory will be mine."

He shook his head. "There is time yet for me to win. I refuse to give up hope."

"I fear you are wasting your energy hoping for something that may never come," I teased.

"The prize is well worth the mental anguish."

He was speaking of the date I'd promised him, contingent on his winning the bet, of course. Suddenly, I found myself wishing he would win, as well. For a moment, I'd considered him as a suspect in the murder. He'd been at the same dinner table as Ruby Stratton, and she had seemed rather fixated on him for at least part of the meal. However, I now had my sights firmly set on Colonel Stratton as the likelier killer.

Mr. Worthing pulled Dr. Rushforth into a conversation concerning his time in the army, and the state of modern medicine, which I was happy to ignore. Lady Dixon had Mrs. Worthing locked into a conversation about the manhandling she received in the Turkish bath.

"The steam room nearly boiled me like a chicken, and my neck is more sore now than it was this morning," she griped.

"I've heard a good massage can make you uncomfortable for a day or two," Mrs. Worthing said. "Isn't that right, Mr. Worthing?"

"All of our best doctors are going to the States." Mr. Worthing was deep into his discussion with Dr. Rushforth, and he didn't seem to even hear his wife. "Next thing you know, we'll all be flying to America for diagnoses."

"I don't think the situation is that dire," Dr. Rushforth said.

"Well, as long as there are doctors like you staying under the crown, I have no reason to worry just yet, I suppose."

Lady Dixon shook her head. "If a massage makes me feel worse than when I went in, it isn't a good massage."

"Mr. Worthing," Mrs. Worthing hissed, elbowing her husband in the side. "What was that you heard about a good massage making you sore immediately after?"

"That a good massage makes you sore immediately after," he said, and then turned back to Dr. Rushforth.

"See, exactly as I said, Lady Dixon." Mrs. Worthing seemed to think Mr. Worthing repeating what she had already said was enough reason for Lady Dixon to believe her. Lady Dixon, however, seemed just as convinced as she was before, which was not in the slightest.

"Regardless, I won't be caught dead in that massage chair again," she said.

The table quieted.

"For goodness sake, are we all going to shy away from anything to do with death because of one murder?" Lady Dixon asked.

Mrs. Worthing laughed, though it sounded stilted and sharp. "Of course not. The conversation simply reached a natural lull. It had nothing to do with what you said."

We all knew Mrs. Worthing had just uttered a bold-faced lie, but it was a comfort, nonetheless. Everyone slipped back into their conversations, and I took the moment to excuse myself. Dr. Rushforth stood to bid me farewell as I pushed in my chair, but otherwise, no one seemed to notice or mind, which suited me just fine.

Since that morning, I'd been thinking of what I'd say to Captain Croft. I'd intended to speak to him prior to break-fast, but the badminton game had taken up more of the day than I'd planned, and my run in with Achilles Prideaux had left me a little deflated. However, with a renewed sense of focus I headed towards the bridge, prepared to finally have some of my burning questions about the murder and my prime suspect answered. Before I made it halfway across the room, though, I saw the Captain walking towards me.

Captain Croft wore a winning smile as he moved through the room, tipping his hat to diners. A few passengers walked up to him and said a few words, but otherwise, the Captain crossed the dining room uninterrupted, his shiny black shoes slapping on the floor. He walked with a purpose—eyes straight ahead, shoulders straight and proud

—which I suspected gave most people the impression that stopping him for a chat about dinner or the weather on deck wouldn't be important enough to disturb him. I wondered whether he practiced the walk or whether it came naturally. The Captain of a ship seemed to be treated similarly to a member of the royal family. Everyone wanted to fawn over him, thanking him for his benevolence, when really it was his job to navigate the ship and lead the passengers from shore to shore safely. With this in mind, I had no qualms about stopping Captain Croft's brisk walk through the dining room.

"Good evening, Captain," I said, side-stepping in front of him as he prepared to brush past me with little more than a glance in my direction.

He came to a stop so suddenly that his head jerked back. It took his eyes several seconds to adjust to my face. When he finally did, I saw his charming smile crumble ever so slightly at the edges.

"Miss Beckingham," he said formally. "Good to see you."

It was apparent he remembered me from the day before, and it was also apparent it was not, in fact, good to see me. He wished to be rid of my presence as soon as possible. He lifted his hand in a quick wave and acted as though he would step around me and be on his way.

"I do wish to apologize for interrupting what appeared to be a rather sensitive meeting yesterday morning," I said quietly, leaning in so he would know I had no intention of sharing the content of the meeting with anyone.

He nodded, his eyes darting around nervously, taking in the group of young women just to his right who stared up at him with stars in their eyes and the elderly couple to the left who kept taking a bite of food and then turning around to openly gawk at the Captain and I as we spoke. Then, he leaned in, as well. "No apology necessary. The conversation, I assure you, was brought on by high emotions and nonsense. No truth to it at all."

"The Colonel was in an extremely fragile state," I said, biting my lower lip and shaking my head slowly. "I assumed he had embellished the truth a bit."

Captain Croft pulled his eyebrows together and tilted his head as he corrected me. "No, Colonel Stratton did not embellish the truth. He fabricated the entire story from start to finish. I had nothing to do with Rose Stratton aside from a brief conversation at dinner. And I shared similar conversations with many other women throughout the evening. I spoke to nearly everyone in the first-class dining room, as you may have noticed."

I placed a reassuring, white-gloved hand on his elbow. "I did notice, and it is nothing to be concerned over. Neither I, nor anyone else, would ever blame you for noticing what any man with eyes was bound to notice—Ruby Stratton was a beautiful woman."

The Captain seemed flustered. His pale face grew blotchy—red patches forming on his neck and cheekbones —and he clenched and unclenched his fists. "There wasn't anything especially attractive...Ruby Stratton was beautiful, yes, but that does not change...she and I barely spoke at all...the two things have nothing to do with one another."

Captain Croft had stepped into the struggle many people found themselves in after tragedy. It felt wrong to criticize the recently deceased, even if that only meant saying she was not as beautiful as people thought her. But in the predicament the Captain found himself in—being charged of a potential crime by the dead woman's husband —he also didn't want to openly admit that he had found her attractive. After several seconds of silent struggle in which his mouth opened to speak, but continually closed when he could not find the words, Captain Croft finally settled on silence.

I could tell he wanted to leave, but being the gentleman he was, he couldn't seem to decide how exactly to extricate himself from the situation.

"I do not believe the Colonel's claims, if that is why you are so anxious to get away," I whispered. "Whether you and Ruby had an attraction to one another is no one's business, especially now that she is gone."

The Captain didn't seem fully at ease, but his lips did soften into an uneasy smile. "Thank you, Miss Beckingham. I can count on your discretion, then?"

"Certainly," I nodded, eyes narrowed to express how seriously I felt about the topic. "I wouldn't wish to get you in any trouble with the ship company or your adoring crew and passengers."

He waved away my compliment, though I could tell he didn't disagree with the truth of it. "Thank you again, Miss. Really."

He made to move past me, but I once again blocked his way. "I do have a few questions for you, if you have a moment."

Captain Croft glanced around the room in search of an excuse to leave, but upon finding none, he sighed and waved for me to continue.

"How was Ruby murdered?" I asked.

This was not the question I'd planned to ask first. I'd thought, perhaps, it would be best to build up to it, but with the Captain finally standing in front of me, willing to answer my questions, I couldn't wait.

"Miss Beckingham," he sighed, shaking his head.

My question was the height of impropriety. Polite society

dictated that conversations should be light and cheerful, or, at the very least, not concern the violent murder of a young woman. I understood that, but I couldn't very well investigate a murder without knowing by which means the victim had been killed. However, I also had to tread carefully. I didn't want Captain Croft to know I'd taken up the investigation. I knew he would frown upon the idea, and then he certainly wouldn't agree to answer any of my questions.

"Please, Captain Croft. She was a friend of mine." A lie, but only in the literal sense of the word 'friend.' Technically, Ruby and I had been introduced to one another at dinner the first night aboard the ship, and she had confided in me only an hour later that she feared for her life. Those series of events hinted at a certain amount of intimacy between us. Of course, I had failed to utilize the information she'd given me to save her, which was precisely the reason I felt compelled to reveal her murderer. Ruby deserved justice, and I would find it for her if I could.

Captain Croft stared at me for a few more seconds, the wheels in his mind turning. Then, he placed a hand on the center of my back and directed me out of the dining room and into the mostly empty corridor.

"If I give you the information you ask for, do you promise to let this go?" he asked.

"*Let this go?*" I repeated. "Ruby Stratton's murder happened two days ago. I don't think wondering how she died is anything out of the ordinary."

His eyes narrowed as though he had caught me in a lie, and I wondered whether the Captain didn't already know about my investigation, after all. Whether he didn't have at least some clue that my interest went beyond having closure. He didn't mention it, though. Instead, he nodded in resignation and leaned in close, so I could feel his warm breath on my cheek.

"Strangulation. Her windpipe was completely crushed."

I gasped, though I didn't know why. Of course, strangulation was a violent way to die, but any kind of murder would have been a violent way to die, regardless. Maybe somehow I'd convinced myself that perhaps Ruby was poisoned. Or the conclusion that she had been murdered was false and she had actually died suddenly of an undiagnosed disease or illness. Learning that she had, without a doubt, been murdered, made me feel slightly nauseous.

"I know," Captain Croft agreed. "Such a violent end to a young woman's life."

"Do you have any suspects?" I asked. I still felt lightheaded from the previous question, but if I let this opportunity pass by, I couldn't be sure I'd have the Captain's ear again.

"I don't think it would be prudent of me to share that information, Miss. I'm sorry."

"I understand," I said. "I'm sure you have an ongoing investigation, correct?"

He nodded, and then looked past me down the hallway, his eyes distant and tired. "I really must be going now, Miss Beckingham."

"Of course," I said, reaching out to brush his starched white jacket. "I only have one more question, if you have the time."

He raised an eyebrow expectantly. Though the Captain oozed charm, I could tell he was growing impatient with me. "Of course, Miss Beckingham."

"Have you been able to discover when Mrs. Stratton was murdered?" I asked.

He crossed his arms over his chest and leaned back, as if

he didn't want anyone who may have been watching our conversation to think we were too friendly with one another. "We don't have an exact timeline, no."

"Any guesses? It doesn't have to be exact," I said.

Captain Croft sighed. "Forgive me, ma'am, but this is not exactly polite conversation. I don't feel right talking about it, and I don't wish to upset you."

I'd asked the question, hadn't I? If the topic would be upsetting to me, I wouldn't have cornered him to discuss it. Lady Dixon had blown up at the dinner table when everyone quieted at her mention of death, and I was beginning to understand her frustration. Of course, speaking of a killing didn't bring joy to my heart. It was uncomfortable and messy and heartbreaking, but it was also a real part of life. Were we expected to ignore the murder of a fellow passenger?

"I know the topic can be rather dark, and I don't wish at all to make you uncomfortable. If your concern is for my wellbeing, let me assure you I can handle the details," I said.

"The topic does not make me uncomfortable," he said, puffing out his chest.

I smiled at him. "Then, we are agreed. The topic does not make either of us any more uncomfortable than is expected when discussing murder. So, if you are ready to tell it, I am ready to hear it."

Captain Croft readjusted his arms and shifted his weight from foot to foot, and I could tell he was wondering whether I hadn't somehow tricked him into answering the question. Still, he gave me the information I wanted. "Lady Dixon was heard shouting for help from the Stern of the ship at six in the morning. When crew members arrived several minutes later, Ruby Stratton's body was chilled, but not yet cold. The ship's physician believed her to be just recently deceased."

"Lady Dixon found the body?" I asked. How had that fact not come up? The topic of Ruby's murder had been raised in conversation several times, yet Lady Dixon never once felt compelled to mention she had discovered the body. That seemed awfully suspicious.

Captain Croft nodded impatiently. "I've seen the Lady and her niece on an early morning walk every day since the ship set sail. They do a full lap of the vessel's deck before breakfast, and once again before lunch."

"And she is not considered a suspect?" I asked, remembering how harshly Lady Dixon had spoken about Ruby after her death. How could she have said so many insensitive things after seeing the poor woman strangled and lying on the deck? The old woman was more of a monster than I'd previously thought, and while I doubted she had the strength to subdue Ruby and crush her windpipe, Jane seemed capable. The question was whether Lady Dixon had enough control over her niece to command a murder on her behalf.

"Once again, I do not feel it is appropriate to discuss such sensitive information with a passenger, miss. I do apologize, but I must be going."

And with that, Captain Croft made his escape. Contrary to his words, he did not seem at all sorry to go. He left rather quickly.

I considered going back in to dinner, but the thought of sitting at the table with all the new information swirling around in my mind, all while the Worthings discussed the benefits of a good massage, seemed unbearable. I turned on my heel and headed down the corridor in the direction of a side stairwell that lead to the deck below. Suddenly, a man stepped out from a doorway to the right and blocked my path. I yelped at his sudden appearance and stepped back.

"My apologies, Mademoiselle."

Achilles Prideaux stood in front of me, his dark eyes sharp and focused. He folded his hands behind his back and stood up straight. "You left suddenly this morning. We did not have a chance to speak."

"I was feeling unwell," I said, repeating the lie I'd told Mrs. Worthing.

He nodded, and it was clear he did not believe me. I hadn't exactly made my feelings about Mr. Prideaux a secret. I did not trust him. In fact, he scared me.

"I'm sorry to hear that, but I'm glad you seem to be feeling better."

"Thank you." I smiled and stepped forward, hoping to move past him and end the conversation. Suddenly, I was feeling bad for cornering Captain Croft. Had he felt this anxious to be out of my presence?

Achilles Prideaux let me pass, which was surprising; however, he immediately fell into step beside me. "I'm heading back to my cabin, as well. Do you mind if I follow you?"

Right. He slept in the cabin across the hall from mine. Something about Achilles Prideaux—whether it was his swarthy appearance or his penchant for showing up everywhere I happened to be, struck me as threatening, so the thought of him sleeping a matter of feet away from me left me uneasy.

"I suppose not," I said, again seeking to make my feelings on the matter known.

My displeasure did not dissuade Monsieur Prideaux. He gestured for me to enter the stairwell first, and then followed behind me. I moved down the stairs faster than normal, thinking at any moment he could shove me from behind and leave me crumpled at the bottom. However, I made it to the bottom safely.

"I wish to offer you a warning," he said in a quiet voice.

"A warning? Have you tired of threats?"

Achilles smiled, and grabbed my arm, pulling me back until I faced him. My heart thundered in my chest. I was alone with a strange man, one who had previously told me he knew I hid secrets. Why had I antagonized him?

Sensing my nervousness, he let me go and stepped away. I pulled my arm in close to my side and pressed myself against the corridor wall, putting as much space between myself and Monsieur Prideaux as possible.

"I never intended to threaten you. I'm sorry it appeared that way. I am simply skilled at detecting deception, and I sense you to be deceptive."

I opened my mouth to protest, but he raised a hand to silence me.

"That is not what I have sought you out to say. I wish to warn you of the dangerous path you have chosen to walk."

I looked up and down the corridor, but Monsieur Achilles Prideaux smiled at me and shook his head. I took that to mean he was not speaking literally.

"I am not here to pry or disturb you, Mademoiselle. I simply feel it is my duty to warn you of the danger you are bringing upon yourself."

Was he speaking of the murder investigation? Or something else...I couldn't be certain, and I did not intend to ask.

"Thank you, Monsieur. I do appreciate it." Lie. "However, I am capable of taking care of myself."

He smiled at me, his mustache stretching wide and thin over his lips. "I thought you would say as much. Then, I shall not disturb you further. Have a lovely evening."

I watched his thin frame move down the hallway and

duck into the cabin across from mine. I waited several seconds before following his path and unlocking the door to my own room.

When Monsieur Achilles Prideaux spoke of danger, was he speaking of the danger he himself posed? I turned the lock, grateful for the reassuring thud of the bolt in the metal door.

11

I rose before the sun, moving around my cabin as quietly as possible so as not to wake Mr. or Mrs. Worthing. Though our individual rooms were separated by a sitting room, the couple were the lightest sleepers I'd ever met. If I so much as sneezed in the night, Mrs. Worthing would be knocking on my door, inquiring whether the onboard doctor should be notified.

The corridor lights were still dim—they wouldn't be switched to full brightness for another hour—and I kept a careful eye on Achilles Prideaux's cabin door as I passed, expecting him to leap out at me any moment. He didn't, of course, and I made it to the deck without seeing another soul.

The cold morning air sliced through my clothes with ease. I'd been expecting a chill, as the Captain had told Mr. Worthing the day before that a Northern wind would move in any day now, but my knitted wool cape did little to protect me. There had been almost no need for a heavy coat in India, and the few I did have were left behind, too large to fit into a steamer trunk. I grabbed the edges of my cape and pulled it tighter around my shoulders. I had on stockings, a navy pleated skirt, white gloves, and a sheer white blouse, but suddenly I was thinking fondly of the 'W' sweater Mrs. Worthing had allowed me to borrow the day before.

I began to question whether Lady Dixon and Jane really would have braved the cold to maintain their routine of a pre-breakfast stroll. Lady Dixon liked to keep a rather tight schedule, but the tip of my nose felt as though it would freeze and break off, so certainly they would have stuck to the interior of the ship. However, no sooner had the thought crossed my mind, than I saw the two women rounding the front corner of the ship and heading towards me. They were still so far away that I wouldn't have normally been able to recognize them from such a distance, but Lady Dixon's bird-like silhouette, along with Jane's small frame hunched against the cold, gave them away.

Lady Dixon wore a deep pile black coat with fur wrapped around the collar and cuffs. She paired this with a matching headwrap. Jane had a green wool coat. Her hands were shoved deep into the pockets, and her bare head was bent down in search of solace from the wind.

I couldn't understand Jane's devotion to Lady Dixon. She was under Lady Dixon's care, I knew, but that didn't explain the fierce loyalty. Especially since the old woman treated the girl scarcely better than a servant. I'd tried to offer Jane several opportunities to, if not rebel, then at least vent about the old woman, but she'd refused me at each turn. For myself, my loyalty would wane the moment I was forced to take a pre-dawn walk during a wind storm.

I could tell by the squishing of her forehead that Lady Dixon was watching me as we neared one another, but when her mouth turned downwards in a scowl, I knew she'd finally recognized me.

"Good morning, Lady Dixon," I shouted, trying to be heard over the wind.

Jane's head shot up. She had been so busy trying to stay warm, she hadn't noticed me until I'd spoken. Her eyes narrowed, and I had no doubt she was wondering what on earth had compelled me to willingly take a stroll in the gale.

Lady Dixon offered me a tight-lipped smile and then faced forward, proceeding on as if I hadn't spoken at all. The polite thing to do, of course, would have been for her to invite me to join them. It was clear that Lady Dixon, however, despite all her self-righteousness and judgments, would do no such thing. So, it would be up to me to invite myself, something I had no problem doing.

"Lovely morning for a walk," I said just as a particularly harsh wind whipped across the deck, sending the flaps of my cape flying into my face. I smoothed them down, managing to keep a straight face.

"I love a morning stroll. It's so *peaceful*," she responded, shooting a sidelong glance at me.

"Absolutely. I've never seen the deck so empty," I said.

"However," she continued, "today's stroll is for a purpose that isn't peaceful in the slightest. I'm still in search of my mother's brooch, so I'm afraid we really must concentrate."

"I thought you said yesterday that you would give up the search? Don't you believe it to have been stolen?" I asked.

Jane looked up at me, unable to believe I'd just questioned Lady Dixon, and her face was redder than normal. It very well could have been from the wind, though. She had such a delicate complexion, I worried she'd become windburned.

Lady Dixon picked up her pace, leaving the poor staring Jane in the dust—she moved quite fast for an elderly woman. I matched her speed, pulling my attention from her young niece, which caused the line between Lady Dixon's eyebrows to deepen with annoyance.

"I do believe it to be stolen, but I must do my due diligence, as well. If I declare it stolen without searching to the best of my ability, then I do myself and my mother a disservice. The brooch is an heirloom, and I can't give it up so easily."

"That is noble of you, Lady. Then I will not disturb your search," I said.

Lady Dixon lifted her head a little higher, proud to have gotten rid of me, no doubt. However, I quickly disappointed her.

"Six eyes are better than four, so I shall join you in the hunt."

"Jane and I take a walk every morning, and we've never seen you up so early." I could hear the judgment in her voice. The first time we'd met, she'd seen me napping on the deck, and then I'd been late to the first evening's dinner. In her mind, I would always be lazy. "What compelled you to do so today?"

"I was having a difficult time sleeping and staying below deck can make me feel so closed in and anxious at times. Ship life really isn't the life for me," I said with a self-deprecating laugh.

We walked in silence for several moments, while I tried to think of how best to begin my line of questioning. I wanted to talk with Lady Dixon about the morning she found Ruby's dead body, but I knew if I didn't approach the subject delicately, there was a chance she would clam up and avoid answering any of my questions.

"Do you remember having your brooch when you found Ruby's body? Perhaps that could help us narrow down where you could have lost it," I said. Then I amended, "Or where it could have been taken."

Lady Dixon sucked in a breath between her teeth, and then clacked her tongue against the roof of her mouth several times. I couldn't be certain that she had been seeking to keep the information a secret, but I did know she hadn't told anyone. And considering she had been part of many conversations that centered around Ruby's death, it seemed surprising she would keep the information to herself. I wanted to find out what she knew, but also why she hadn't offered up this key part of the story.

"I had the brooch when Jane and I left our cabin that morning for our walk. I did not take notice or think of it again until it was already gone," she said, her words clipped and sharp. More than ever, Lady Dixon did not wish to speak to me, but if I let that deter me, I would never have spoken to her in the first place.

"I'm sure finding the body was quite a shock. Perhaps you lost the brooch in the rush to check if Ruby Stratton was still alive," I said. Framing the question around the missing brooch seemed like the surest method of both sounding concerned and uncovering more information about Ruby Stratton's murder. The only person aside from the Captain and the murderer, that I knew of, who had been at the scene of the crime was Lady Dixon and Jane. Of course, there was always the possibility they were also the murderers, which was precisely what I hoped to find out.

"I was not involved in that process. I am neither a doctor nor a detective. Therefore, I had no business touching a body, and I did no such thing," Lady Dixon said, her nose turned up.

"You mean to say, you found a fellow human lying unconscious on the deck and did nothing to assist them?" I asked, looking from the old woman to her young niece. I'd been asking questions to satisfy my investigation, but suddenly I found myself asking them from sheer curiosity. How could a person find a body and yet not consider themselves involved?

"Ruby Stratton was beyond assistance," Lady Dixon said coolly. I had to wonder whether there weren't two meanings hidden behind her words.

"You were not aware of that at the time of her discovery, though. Correct?"

Captain Croft said Ruby Stratton's death had been caused by strangulation—a crushed windpipe. It was a less obvious kind of death. Unlike gunfire or a knife blade, strangulation caused no obvious signs of trauma. Nothing that would cause someone to scream in horror and run for help. No blood or horrific gaping wounds. Ruby Stratton, aside from some bruising around the neck and popped vessels in her eyes, would have looked unharmed from a distance.

And Lady Dixon, with the low opinion she already had of Mrs. Stratton, certainly would have assumed she had become too drunk to walk back to her cabin before even entertaining the possibility of murder. Most normal people, I've found, seek the most improbable conclusions before allowing themselves to believe a person could actually be dead. Death is a wholly unnatural phenomenon that, despite how many people do it every day, is still an utter surprise each and every time. Lady Dixon would have been surprised. At least, she should have been.

Lady Dixon was bent forward, checking underneath a built-in bench for her missing brooch, and did not answer me right away. I did not repeat my question, however, as the tension in her shoulders told me she had heard it just fine. When she rose back to standing, she glanced over at me, and upon seeing my expectant expression, she took a deep breath and answered.

"I do not intend to cross into a sensitive topic," Lady Dixon said, though the slight smile on her lips said otherwise. "But you have been in the company of dead bodies before, haven't you? Quite recently, in fact?"

She knew I had. The first evening at dinner we had discussed the explosion—the death of the whole Beckingham family, aside from myself. Lady Dixon hoped I'd respond as I had that first night. She hoped I would excuse myself, cheeks red and eyes glassy with unshed tears. She hoped I would leave her alone and drop my line of questioning. As much as I wanted to, even as my throat closed with the memory of the stench and my eyes watered at the thought of the smoke, I would not flee. I would not run away from the horrors of my past anymore. I would face them down, just as Lady Dixon would have to face down her own.

"You are correct, my Lady," I said, my voice as calm and even as I could manage.

"Then surely, you, more than anyone, can understand the difference between a live body and a dead one," Lady Dixon said, her face pulled taut.

"Forgive me, Lady, but in the instance you are referring to, death was the expected outcome. I did not have to wonder whether those around me were dead or alive because it was obvious that everyone in the vehicle, myself included, should have been dead. Seeing a dead body on a morning stroll, however, seems to warrant a different response."

I couldn't help myself, I was losing my cool. Lady Dixon had struck me almost immediately as a hard woman, but it wasn't until that moment that I'd considered her a cruel one. She spoke easily of something I wouldn't even be able to think on for more than a few minutes at a time without becoming emotional. How could I be expected to remain neutral in the face of such heartlessness?

"This is an awfully dark topic for so early in the morning," Lady Dixon responded. "It's not suitable for young Jane."

Jane's face flushed, and I wondered whether it was out of embarrassment or from the chill. Lady Dixon expected the young girl to act like a woman, yet now she wanted to use her youthfulness to avoid my inquiries.

"Yes, I'm so sorry, Jane," I said, slowing down to let Lady Dixon pass by so Jane and I could walk together. "It must have been difficult to find Ruby Stratton in that state."

She looked up at me as though no one had ever spoken directly to her, as if she didn't know what to do with the attention.

"Yes, it was a horrible sight to—"

"Jane stood behind me. She hardly saw a thing," Lady Dixon said harshly, turning around, her hawk-like eyes focused on the young girl.

Jane closed her mouth tightly, looking up at me for only a moment before casting her gaze back to the ground.

"Besides," Lady Dixon continued, "we did not learn that the deceased was Ruby Stratton until hours later, at the same time as the rest of the ship."

"How is that possible?" I asked.

I had joined the two women at the front of the ship, but we were now near the stern. If Captain Croft's information was to be believed, Lady Dixon and Jane would make one full loop of the ship before moving to the dining room for breakfast. I could still talk with Lady Dixon over breakfast, of course, but it would be much easier for her to avoid me with the presence of the other passengers.

Lady Dixon sighed. "Much as it is now, the sun had barely risen. The deck was cast in harsh light and shadows, and Ruby Stratton's body had been stuffed into an area of shadow beneath some wicker deck furniture. It was lucky I noticed her at all. My vision has always been sharp and has not diminished a bit with age, so I saw her well before Jane did, distracted as she was by our run-in with Dr. Rushforth."

"You saw Dr. Rushforth that morning?" I asked.

Lady Dixon continued without pause. "I was instructing Jane that etiquette dictated she should make eye contact with those she is in conversation with, and that she ought not to hide behind me. As I was speaking, I looked over and saw a bare foot sticking out from beneath the chair."

Jane, clearly not heeding the advice the old woman had offered her that morning, was shrinking behind Lady Dixon, looking as though she wished she could seep into the wooden floor. I looked to her, hoping she would answer my question.

"Dr. Rushforth was on the deck that morning?" I asked.

Jane nodded her head ever so slightly. So subtly, in fact, I couldn't even be sure it was a head nod. Luckily, Lady Dixon finally decided to answer my question.

"Yes, he told us he had just finished responding to a female passenger with a sick infant. The Captain called upon him to assist her while the ship's doctor was preoccupied with another ill passenger."

I'd seen Dr. Rushforth that morning and he hadn't mentioned anything about assisting with a sick passenger. However, that information would have seemed inconsequential in the face of the news of Ruby Stratton's death. Besides, it was very likely he had no knowledge of being so near the body prior to discovery. I replayed the conversation I'd had with him that fateful morning, searching my memory for any important details, anything I could use to cross-reference with Lady Dixon.

Dr. Rushforth had said he'd gone to see the Captain the moment he heard of the death but could be of no assistance because Ruby Stratton had been dead for quite some time. Immediately, Captain Croft's words the night before rang once again in my head. *Ruby Stratton's body was chilled, but not yet cold. The ship's physician believed her to be just recently deceased.*

"How long had Ruby Stratton been dead when you discovered her body?" I asked.

"Apparently, the murder had occurred quite recently. Jane and I stayed—keeping our distance, of course—until the Captain and several crew members could arrive. They said her body still maintained a touch of warmth. We are lucky we arrived when we did. If we had taken our walk only half an hour earlier, we could have stumbled upon a rather ghastly scene," Lady Dixon said.

Colonel Stratton, as I'd learned two nights before, had returned to his cabin near three in the morning, and I'd seen him close to seven. If Lady Dixon found the body between six and seven, and the body had only recently been deceased. Colonel Stratton would have had to leave his room in the wee hours of the morning, having had no sleep, kill his wife on the deck, and then return to his room without being spotted by anyone so he could answer the door at seven when the crew member knocked to deliver the news. All of that, though possible, seemed unlikely.

The Colonel had been my main suspect since I'd first heard of the murder, but suddenly I had evidence that provided reasonable doubt. Even with the timeline fleshed out, however, I was hesitant to eliminate him as a suspect. His behavior surrounding the murder seemed erratic.

Dr. Rushforth, who I had all but eliminated, now seemed to be rising to the forefront of the investigation. Had Dr. Rushforth been misinformed about the time of Ruby's death or had he spread the lie purposely? That question was now the most important one to answer. With her testimony, Lady Dixon had just placed the Doctor near the scene of the crime minutes before the body was discovered, and Dr. Rushforth had quickly sought to involve himself in the investigation. Was that in an effort to cast suspicion away from himself or out of the goodness of his heart?

What purpose could he have for harming Ruby Stratton, though? I'd noticed an odd dynamic between him and Ruby Stratton at dinner the night before the murder, but nothing that seemed volatile enough to lead to murder. Dr. Rushforth, like most men, had seemed simply to notice Ruby's beauty and appreciate it, but that was hardly cause for murder.

While my mind whirled with thoughts of Dr. Rushforth, I had to wonder whether I wasn't overlooking a more obvious suspect. Had I, like Thomas Arbuckle, assumed the murderer was a man? Lady Dixon and Jane had been the two to find Ruby's body, and unlike Dr. Rushforth, they knew Ruby prior to boarding the ship. Suddenly, I remembered the letter in the bottom of the Strattons' trunk.

"In the time you knew Ruby Stratton, did you ever hear her mention someone by the name of 'Mo Mo?'" I asked.

Lady Dixon seemed jarred by this line of questioning. She reared back her head, eyebrows furrowed. "That is hardly a name," she said, lip curled, and then she shook her head. "I never heard any mention of such a person."

I was going to thank Lady Dixon and Jane for their time, as I knew we were nearing the end of their walk, but before I could, Lady Dixon came to a sudden stop. Jane nearly crashed into the woman's back, though she managed to stop herself just in time.

"This is where we must part, Miss Beckingham," Lady Dixon said. "Good day."

She turned on her heel and marched away before I could say another word, which suited me just fine. I had a lot to digest. At every turn, it seemed as though I was gathering more information, but getting further and further away from a clear answer.

The sun had fully risen, washing the deck in golden light. I knew breakfast would start any minute. Passengers were pouring up the stairs from the decks below. I, however, moved against the current, climbing down the stairs to return to my cabin. I no longer felt capable of eating.

Luckily, by the time I returned to the room, Mr. and Mrs. Worthing had already left, which meant they would not come looking for me until after breakfast. I lay back on my bed, cape fanning out around my face, with my arms crossed over my chest.

I needed to uncover which passenger Dr. Rushforth had been assisting that morning. It would help to establish a timeline for his whereabouts. I had as much information as I was likely to get about where Colonel Stratton and Lady Dixon and Jane were during the time Ruby Stratton was murdered. The investigation now would be a game of elimination. Who had been in the right place at the right time? Or, in Ruby Stratton's case, the wrong place at the wrong time?

As I was thinking, I heard a scraping noise near the corner of my room. I sat up immediately, looking around. When I'd come into the room, I hadn't turned on the main light, opting instead for the lamp next to the bed, so the room was dim. Because of that, it took me several seconds to notice the square shape on the floor in front of the door. I slipped out of bed and walked to it. It was a note. And the sound I'd heard had been the paper sliding under the door.

Before reading the note, I pulled the door open quickly, and stepped into the corridor. It was empty and quiet, not a peep or whisper of movement. I waited several seconds to be sure no one was hiding around the corner. When I felt confident I was alone, I shut the door and unfolded the note.

In sloppy, scribbled handwriting were these words:

Meet in the maintenance closet behind the stairs on Deck E.

12

I hesitated only a few seconds before checking my makeup and the appearance of my scar in the washroom mirror and then leaving my cabin, the note clutched in my hand.

There seemed to be no other option than to meet with whoever had written the note. I knew it was dangerous. The note writer could be the same person who murdered Ruby. She had been only next door, after all. Perhaps my investigation was entirely off base and the murderer had been someone Ruby didn't know at all, who had drawn her from her room with the use of a vague note. Or—and this was the option I hoped for—the note was written by someone who had information that could be useful for my investigation. And it was that option which drew me from my room and had me standing on the landing of Deck E, searching for a maintenance closet.

Deck E was reserved for the lower classes. Cabin doors studded the corridor walls at regular intervals, showcasing how small each cabin was. Every sixth door was labeled "communal lavatory." I shuddered at the mere thought of sharing a washroom with five other families.

Just behind the staircase, exactly where the note said it would be, was a maintenance closet. The crack under the door looked dark and there was no window set into the door, meaning I would get no clue of what was on the other side until it was too late to turn back. My heart began to pound in my chest, beating out a warning. *Turn back – turn back – turn back.*

As much as I wanted to listen to it, I pushed the thought away. If I walked away now, I would make myself sick with regret. What if I'd walked away from information that could have solved the case? Besides, if there was someone set on killing me hiding behind the door, they would find an opportunity eventually. It was better to face it head on now than to sit in fear and uncertainty.

Before I could talk myself out of it, I lifted a fist and rapped on the door three times.

Nothing happened for a few seconds. I even began to wonder whether I hadn't beat the person who'd written the note to the closet. Then, without warning, the door was thrown open and a hand wrapped itself around my arm and pulled me into the closet. I yelped with surprise.

"It is only me, miss."

The soft voice. The sing-song accent. The small, shadowy figure.

"Aseem," I breathed, relief flooding through me. "You frightened me."

I had almost forgotten about the young boy stowed away in the cargo hold. I'd asked him to use his ability to move quietly and hide to assist me, but we had been interrupted before I could give him any kind of specific instruction. Both how he had discovered which cabin was mine and what he had to say to me was a total mystery. I was briefly impressed, not only by his stealth, but by the education of the child who could speak and write in my language as well as his own. Then, he broke into my thoughts.

"I am sorry," he said. "It is dangerous for me to be seen by anyone."

"Then why have you taken such a great risk by delivering the note and meeting me?" I asked.

I wanted to turn on a light, to illuminate the dark space and see the young boy's face, but even in the gloom, I could see Aseem shake his head from side to side when I swiped the wall in search of a light switch.

"I have some information you may find useful," he said.

"And what would that be?" I asked, still uncertain. How would Aseem have any idea what information would be useful to me?

"I overheard your conversation with Lady Dixon on the deck this morning, and—"

"What? How?" I asked, interrupting him. Lady Dixon had been moving at a rather quick pace, and as far as I knew, we were the only people on the deck. To follow us, Aseem would have needed to be in constant motion and remain unseen. It was a near-impossible task.

"No matter, miss. I overheard Lady Dixon tell you the Doctor had visited a sick infant just before running into her on the deck?"

"Dr. Rushforth. Yes, that is what she said." Until he had given specifics of the conversation I'd shared with Lady Dixon, I'd still doubted whether Aseem was telling the truth about overhearing us. Now, though, there was almost no doubt. "How were you able to follow us?"

Aseem shook his head at my question and then looked

up at me, his eyes white and sparkling despite the dark. "It was a lie."

"What was a lie? What Lady Dixon said?"

"Dr. Rushforth lied to the Lady. He did visit an infant in the early morning, but it was near three that morning, not just before Ruby's body was discovered," he said.

"How can you know this, Aseem?"

He smiled. "In the same way I know what you spoke to Lady Dixon about. And the same way I knew which cabin you are staying in."

Part of me felt uneasy at the thought of being observed by Aseem without my knowledge. However, a larger part was focused on the information he had been able to gather.

"So, you are saying Dr. Rushforth was unaccounted for between visiting the infant at three and seeing Lady Dixon and Jane at seven?" I asked.

Aseem nodded, his lips sucked in, eyes wide.

"Do you understand what this information means?" I asked. I had not told Aseem about my investigation, and even though his information was quite pertinent, he could have simply shared it because of the conversation he'd overheard me having with Lady Dixon.

"If you are asking whether or not I know why you are asking so many questions, the answer is yes. You are not as careful as you think you are, Miss Beckingham," Aseem said.

I wanted to be offended by Aseem's criticism of me, but it was impossible. He spoke with so much frankness and honestly, that I could only smile. "I suppose you are the master of subtlety."

He nodded. "It is one of my skills, yes."

The boy seemed to know something about everyone of importance on the ship, so it seemed a waste not to utilize his knowledge. "Can you tell me anything about Achilles Prideaux?"

Aseem screwed up his face in thought, and then shrugged his shoulders. "Not much. But I do believe you can trust him."

"Really?" I asked, surprised. Perhaps, Aseem had not observed Monsieur Prideaux closely enough to make out his true character. I would take his opinion into consideration but would ultimately have to follow my own instincts.

The boy nodded. "I must be going. It will be easier to move unnoticed while most of the passengers are at breakfast."

"I don't want to risk you being discovered, but will you inform me if you uncover any information that is pertinent to the investigation?" It felt odd to ask a child for assistance, but Aseem was wise beyond his years. I didn't know what traumas had lead him to stow away on the ship, but I imagined, like myself, that he felt leaving India was his best chance at a new life.

Aseem cracked the door open, light from the hallway cutting across the small closet and casting his face in a harsh line. In the light, I could see him turn his gaze to me and nod once. Then, he poked his head into the hallway, and upon seeing it empty, slipped from the room and closed the door behind him. I waited several seconds before following him, and once I did, the hallway was empty. Aseem had disappeared.

13

D r. Rushforth had lied about his whereabouts the morning of Ruby Stratton's murder. Or Lady Dixon had misunderstood. Either way, the facts were this: Dr. Rushforth was out of his cabin and unaccounted for between three and seven in the morning, and Ruby Stratton was killed between five and seven.

After meeting with Aseem, I returned once again to my cabin, hoping for a few moments of peace. I'd woken unusually early to intercept Lady Dixon and Jane on their walk and Aseem had interrupted my first attempt at a nap when he delivered his note. I felt long overdue for some rest, however, Mrs. Worthing knocked on the door the moment I'd laid my head down. I groaned, rose to my feet, and fully accepted that I would not get any rest until that evening —if then.

I opened the door only a crack, but Mrs. Worthing pushed it open with both hands, bursting into my room without a second thought for my privacy. I was momentarily pinned between the back side of the door and the wall.

"We missed you at dinner, dear. You are feeling all

right?" she asked, resting on the edge of my bed, fidgeting with the unmade blankets. She wore a pale pink tea dress with a pleated skirt and a bucket hat, a matching ribbon wrapped around the base. The color was pretty, but it washed her out. She looked pink all over, like a salmon that had jumped from the ocean and landed on the deck.

I closed the door and nodded. "You are so kind to worry, but I am perfectly healthy. Just a little tired is all."

"Lady Dixon said you accompanied her and Jane on their walk this morning," Mrs. Worthing said, her voice slightly higher than normal. She exhaled deeply.

"Yes, we had a rather long conversation while we walked," I said. "Did you know they were the ones who found Ruby Stratton's body on deck?"

Mrs. Worthing looked away from me, giving her full attention to a blank space on the cabin wall. "Yes," she said with a jerk of her head. "I'd heard that."

So perhaps Lady Dixon discovering Ruby's body wasn't such a secret after all. Maybe Lady Dixon had simply not mentioned the topic while I was present. It wasn't difficult to imagine. I saw the Lady and Jane at meal times, but otherwise we seemed to occupy different parts of the ship.

"I only just heard the news this morning. Shocking, isn't it?"

Mrs. Worthing shrugged her shoulders and scuffed the toe of her black Mary Jane into the wooden floor. "Not so shocking. Lady Dixon seems to know everything there is to know before everyone else. I would have assumed she'd told you about finding Mrs. Stratton, considering you two are so close now."

It was then that I realized how sub-par my investigative skills truly were. Mrs. Worthing was jealous. She believed me to prefer the company of Lady Dixon over herself, which seemed an absurd conclusion to reach, given the fact that Lady Dixon was one of the most insufferable people I'd ever encountered in my entire life.

"My running into her this morning was a total accident," I rushed to explain. "I can assure you, I would not have sought out Lady Dixon on my own. The woman shares her opinions too freely, occasionally venturing into cruelty."

Mrs. Worthing tore her eyes away from the interesting blank canvas of my wall to look up at me. Her eyebrows were still lowered and drawn together, hesitant to trust what I was saying. "You didn't plan to meet with her for a walk this morning?"

"Absolutely not," I said with more passion than necessary. "I couldn't sleep, so I wandered up on deck, and we ran into one another. It felt rude not to join them, which is the only reason I did so. Honestly, it felt like a waste of a good walk, but social etiquette rules us all."

Mrs. Worthing laughed. "That it does, my dear. I'm actually glad you said something, because Lady Dixon had said several things that have given me pause. She spoke so harshly of Ruby Stratton after her murder, and I found Mrs. Stratton to be a remarkably sweet woman."

"I didn't know Ruby well enough to make any judgments on her, but she hardly seemed deserving of the criticism Lady Dixon hurled at her," I agreed.

"I promised Ruby I would tell no one, but now that she is dead, it hardly seems a secret," Mrs. Worthing said, leaning forward slightly and lowering her voice. "I caught Mrs. Stratton sitting on the deck the evening before her murder, writing in a notebook. She was drafting a letter to someone named Mo Mo."

My heart seized in my chest, and suddenly Mrs. Worthing had my full and undivided attention.

"I came up behind her and remarked on what an unusual name it was, and Mrs. Stratton nearly jumped out of her skin. She closed the notebook quickly and begged me to mention nothing of it to the Colonel. I told her I would say nothing, though I did press her to give me more information. All she would say was that Mo Mo was a correspondence she had kept for nine years—a destitute young woman to whom she sent money and encouragement via letters. I told her she needn't keep her charity from her husband, but she insisted he was to know nothing of it."

"So, you have no idea who Mo Mo is, aside from the little information she shared with you?" I asked, desperate to know more.

Mrs. Worthing shook her head. "No, she revealed nothing else. But Ruby's humbleness was inspiring. She simply wished to help poor Mo Mo out, and didn't want even her husband to know of her good deed. Most people, you know, seek glory wherever they can. But not Ruby Stratton."

"Noble, indeed," I said.

Despite being able to convince Mrs. Worthing of her charitable nature, Ruby Stratton had never struck me as a giver. She was a young woman, married to a well to do older man, with an eye for attractive men. She seemed like the kind of person who enjoyed a fast, fun life. Not the kind of woman who would spend her energy sending extra pocket money to a poor young woman she'd once met. So, that begged the question, who was Mo Mo to Ruby Stratton? And why would Ruby wish to keep her identity secret from her husband? And what, if anything, did Mo Mo have to do with Ruby's murder?

The clock in my room struck nine, and Mrs. Worthing

jumped to her feet with a yelp. "Oh, I nearly forgot why I'd come in the first place. I signed us up for a dancing class."

I was already shaking my head before she could finish. "Mrs. Worthing, I really shouldn't. I'm a horrible dancer. It simply isn't in my bones."

"Nonsense," the woman said, looping her arm through mine and pulling me towards the door. "You are young and fit and beautiful. All a woman needs to do to be considered a good dancer is be pretty enough to catch the eye of a gentleman. He will lead you around the room, requiring little to no effort on your part."

"But I don't have the right clothes for dancing," I said in a desperate attempt to avoid the embarrassment that certainly awaited me.

"The dress you have on is fine," she said, already opening my cabin door and pulling me into the hallway. "Besides, it's a beginner's class. No one will judge you if you are wearing the wrong kind of shoes."

I wanted to argue more, but I knew it would do no good. Just as I had given up on taking a nap, I gave up on the idea of getting out of the dance class. Mrs. Worthing's will was much greater than my own. So, I quit dragging my feet and let myself be pulled along, all the way to the gymnasium.

14

The gymnasium was much larger than I expected. It was at least six times the length of the sitting room I shared with the Worthings and had a wall of floor to ceiling windows on one side, offering a spectacular view of the ocean. When Mrs. Worthing and I arrived to the class, despite Mrs. Worthing's insistence that we were severely late, everyone was gathered around the window.

"There you are, dear," Mr. Worthing said, grabbing Mrs. Worthing's arm and spinning her easily enough that I suspected they were slightly more advanced than the beginner's level. "I worried you had found another partner and decided to stand me up."

Mrs. Worthing waved away his banter and smoothed down her skirts. "Rose and I started talking and I got distracted."

"Glad to see you, Rose," Mr. Worthing said, leaning around his wife to look at me. "We missed you at breakfast."

"Yes, I didn't sleep well last night, and I—"

I didn't bother finishing my sentence. Just then, a

woman, who I presumed to be the teacher of the class, clapped her hands twice, drawing the attention of everyone in the room. Mr. and Mrs. Worthing clasped hands and hurried to the center of the room, leaving me all alone.

"Welcome dancers, I am Mrs. Kinney, and I will be your dance instructor today."

The woman had short dark hair that was smoothed back on her head with subtle finger waves framing her face. She wore a drop waist dress with a handkerchief hem that was absolutely doused in glitter. Every inch of her seemed to sparkle gold, from her t-strap heels all the way to her sequined headband.

The crowd in front of her mumbled a collective greeting, which seemed to satisfy Mrs. Kinney well enough to carry on.

"Now, if everyone could partner up, we will jump right in," she said, extending her hand out to the man standing beside her, who I hadn't noticed at all only a moment prior, but I now suspected to be Mr. Kinney.

A wave of panic filled me suddenly. I didn't have a partner. Mrs. Worthing had brought me along, but she had Mr. Worthing, and I had no one. Everyone had come in pairs— the elderly couple to my right who were already wrapped around one another doing a form of ballroom dancing across the floor and the middle-aged couple to my left who looked as though they were in the middle of a fight, whispering to one another from between gritted teeth. I took a step backwards towards the door. Mrs. Worthing was distracted enough by Mr. Worthing that certainly she wouldn't notice my absence for a good long while. And when she confronted me about it later, I could come up with an excuse or tell her the truth. Actually, the truth could work well. She would feel guilty enough for bringing me along without a partner, that she would forgive me for slipping away unnoticed. Settled on that plan, I turned on my heel to head for the door.

Immediately, however, I found myself face to face with Dr. Rushforth.

"I see you are in need of a partner, Miss Beckingham." He bowed low, holding his hand up to me as though I were royalty.

Not knowing what to say, I simply grabbed his hand and let him lead me to the dance floor.

I'd been thinking about Dr. Rushforth all morning, planning what I would say to him, how I would ask him about his comings and goings the morning of Ruby Stratton's murder. Running into him unexpectedly, however, had thrown me off my game. Suddenly, I couldn't formulate the thoughts or words necessary to interrogate him.

"We will start with the Fox Trot," Mrs. Kinney called out, pointing at a crew member in the corner to start the music.

She and the man I presumed to be her husband stepped towards one another. Her right hand grasped his left and their spare hands found their partner's waist.

"Many people in my classes come to me and complain that they cannot dance, that they do not have rhythm or talent. So, I teach them the Fox Trot. It is a step everyone can do."

She counted to four, matching the beat of the music, and then she and her partner began to move together stepping on the beat. They stayed within the same area on the dance floor, but they spun and twirled and circled around one another.

"It looks lovely, but the move is as simple as walking. If

you can walk, you can Fox Trot. Please, everyone find your partner and give it a try," she said, breaking away from her own partner to move around the couples, instructing them and giving pointers.

"I'm not much of a dancer. I do hope you'll forgive me in advance for stepping on your feet," Dr. Rushforth said, winking at me.

Before I had time to respond, he grabbed my hand again, wrapped his arm around my waist, and began leading me around the room. I didn't even have to think. Dr. Rushforth gently pushed and pulled on my hips, directing me where I ought to go. I supposed Mrs. Worthing was on to something. All a woman really needed to do was find a good partner.

"You are too modest, Dr. Rushforth. You seem like a fine dancer to me," I said as we made our second lap around the room.

He shrugged. "Fine compared to some, I suppose," he said, nodding his head in the direction of a young couple who were receiving a fair amount of instruction from Mrs. Kinney. The man stomped his foot in frustration when Mrs. Kinney stopped them for a third time to cut in, attempting to show the man how to confidently lead his female partner.

We danced in silence for several minutes, speaking only when the dance instructor finally made her way over to use. She eyed us for a moment, and then nodded approvingly before gliding away. Then, Dr. Rushforth broke the quiet.

"Ruby Stratton seems to have been nearly forgotten," he said.

"What?" I asked, startled by his mention of the dead woman. I had been trying to come up with a subtle way to bring her into the conversation so I could question him, but he had done it for me.

"I believe I will win our bet. Does tonight work for dinner?" he asked with a smile.

Our bet. Yes, of course. I'd nearly forgotten about it yet again. "Not so quickly, Doctor. I spoke with Lady Dixon about the murder only this morning. Not everyone has forgotten."

Dr. Rushforth shrugged, suddenly not as eager to continue the discussion.

"Actually," I said. "She told me this morning that it was she and Jane who discovered Ruby's body. Did you know that?"

He raised his eyebrows in a surprise that didn't seem all that convincing. "I didn't. That must have been a shock."

"Oh, it was. I can't even imagine seeing such a thing," I said, shaking my head, allowing for a slight pause. "In fact, according to Lady Dixon, you missed the moment of discovery by a matter of minutes."

"Is that right?" he asked, his voice cold.

"You did run into Lady Dixon and Jane on the deck that morning, correct?"

He furrowed his brow for a moment as we continued to dance. His hand slipped from mine slightly, his arm loosening around my waist. "Yes, I do believe it was the very same morning."

Mr. and Mrs. Worthing were twirling circles around everyone else on the dance floor, barely following the steps of the Fox Trot. Mrs. Kinney, it appeared, had given up reprimanding them and had decided to let them have their fun.

"If you don't mind me asking, what were you doing up so early? I joined Lady Dixon this morning on her walk, and I can barely keep my eyes open now," I said, letting out a small laugh. "It's a wonder I haven't collapsed into your arms."

"You would not offend me at all if you wished to collapse, Miss Beckingham," Dr. Rushforth said, a smile stretched across his face. Suddenly, his normally sharp features looked more sinister.

"Do not distract me," I said, teasing him. I tried to remain playful, though the dance class had taken on an air of danger. "What had you out of bed so early in the morning? Most people use a long voyage such as this one to relax. Lady Dixon is one of the few people I know regimented enough to rise early each morning for exercise."

"I couldn't distract you even if I wished to." I couldn't help but notice he sounded slightly annoyed, as if he indeed did wish to distract me. "Unfortunately, doctors rarely have the luxury of a holiday. Someone is always coming down ill with something or other."

"So, you were caring for an ill passenger?" I asked.

He shook his head. "An infant. Poor thing had been running a fever for a full day before her mother contacted the ship's doctor. He was busy with a severe case of sea sickness, though. The Captain thought of me and sent a crew member to my cabin."

"Everyone!" Mrs. Kinney clapped twice and the music cut off. "You all made quick work of the Fox Trot, so I'd like to work on something a bit more contemporary."

A few groans came from the surrounding couples, but Mrs. Kinney was not deterred. She and her husband began running through the steps for the next dance. I couldn't focus enough to learn which dance it was, though. Dr. Rushforth had become my main focus.

"You are a kind man to assist someone so early in the morning," I said.

He shrugged and whispered back, "It was not so early."

"Near three in the morning, I heard."

He stiffened slightly at my words. "Yes, I suppose it was near three. By the time I finished, however, I felt wide awake. I wandered the deck for hours waiting for breakfast, unable to sleep."

"Then you must have passed by the spot where Ruby was discovered countless times. It took Lady Dixon and I less than half an hour to circle the entire ship this morning."

He put on a thoughtful face, focusing especially hard on Mr. and Mrs. Kinney as they walked everyone through the steps to the new dance.

"So sad about her death," I said.

"Yes, it is. Death is always a sad affair. And I would know; I've seen an awful lot of it." His words were clipped and sharp, matching the expression in his eyes.

"Oh yes, of course," I said, placing a hand on his arm in apology. "But I learned just today how kind Ruby Stratton was. Do you know she gave of her own fortune to help a young woman less fortunate than herself?"

"Oh?"

I nodded and leaned in to whisper in his ear. "Apparently it was a big secret, but I discovered she was sending her money to a woman, Mo Mo, who needed it. Ruby bought her a coat just last winter," I said, remembering the letter I'd found in the Stratton's trunk.

Dr. Rushforth's face shifted from green to red and back again. I wondered whether he wouldn't be sick.

"Now, you all try," Mrs. Kinney said, clapping twice for the music to begin. A jazzy tune began to play, filling the room with horns and rhythm.

I reached for Dr. Rushforth's hand as all the other couples began to dance, but he took a step away from me.

"I'm sorry, Miss Beckingham, but you'll have to excuse me," he said.

"Is everything all right, Doctor?" I asked.

But Dr. Rushforth did not hear me. He was already halfway across the dance floor.

15

D r. Rushforth did not make an appearance at lunch or dinner, and Mrs. Worthing's anger at his abandoning me at dance class began to shift into concern.

"Did he seem ill when he left the class?" she asked. "Doctors expose themselves to so many diseases. I worry he has fallen ill. We should really find out whether he is sick. Rose spent the morning pressed against him dancing. Who knows what she has been exposed to?"

"He seemed perfectly fine," I said, trying to calm the fears of the table and make them stop eyeing me as though I could be infectious. In all honesty, however, the doctor had seemed anything but fine. He'd been flustered by my line of questioning, and eager to escape. Especially at the mention of Mo Mo.

I'd thrown the name out on a whim, curious to see if there could be a connection between Ruby Stratton's secret correspondent and Dr. Rushforth. His reaction told me there was, though I didn't yet know how.

The investigation seemed to work that way. Each time I

uncovered a clue or found an answer, ten more questions arose. I was wading through an endless sea of information, and I had to pick out the important bits, which at the moment seemed to be the identity of Mo Mo and Dr. Rushforth's relationship with Ruby Stratton. The sooner I answered those questions, the closer I'd be to solving who murdered Ruby Stratton and why.

"The doctor is probably comforting Colonel Stratton," Mr. Worthing said, spooning a steaming mound of green beans into his mouth.

This caught my attention. "Comforting Colonel Stratton?"

Mr. Worthing looked up at me over his plate, nodding as if it were the most obvious thing in the world. "Of course. They've been friends for years and the man's wife was just murdered."

No one at the table seemed surprised by this information, so my shock made me feel daft. "How do you know they've been friends for years?"

"Really, Rose," Mrs. Worthing said, shaking her head. "How have you spent so much time with the Doctor and yet learned nothing about him? He served in the war with Colonel Stratton. He told us so the first night we met."

"I knew he'd been an army surgeon, but I didn't know he knew the Strattons," I said.

"Well, he did," she said. "They served together and, after the war, he and the Strattons lived closely together in Bombay for years."

Ruby's nervous glances at Dr. Rushforth the first night aboard the ship suddenly took on a whole new meaning. They'd known one another prior to boarding. Perhaps I would have picked up on their connection had Lady Dixon not distracted me by talk of the explosion in Simla. I'd been flustered and overwhelmed, eager to leave. My senses were muddled. But now, sharpened by hindsight, I could see how nervous Rose felt around Dr. Rushforth. I replayed the conversation over in my head and stuck on the final moments of dinner.

The Colonel voiced his intent to go to the smoking lounge and remain there until late in the evening. Ruby had been uncomfortable with the idea, even going as far as to ask whether she could accompany him. All of this had happened in front of Dr. Rushforth, who then knew Ruby would be alone in her room, and he almost certainly knew the Colonel would come home tired and drunk. That established an opportunity, but the motive remained just out of reach.

When the conversation switched to the temperature of the indoor swimming pool, I found it impossible to remain an active part of the table's conversation, instead choosing to wander the deck with my thoughts.

"Are you leaving, Rose?" Mrs. Worthing asked as I slid my chair away from the table and stood up.

I nodded. "I'd like to take a stroll around the deck before retiring for the evening."

"You haven't even touched your dessert."

"Mr. Worthing can have mine if he'd like. I am too full to even think of it," I said.

Mrs. Worthing seemed prepared to keep arguing, but Mr. Worthing had already swapped his empty plate for my full one and now he dove in with an eager spoon.

Dinner lasted longer than usual, so the sun had already sunk below the horizon by the time I stepped onto the deck. People milled about here and there, but most everyone had settled inside for the evening, either in the smoking lounge, tea room, or their own cabins. I couldn't blame them. The cool wind from that morning had not relented all day, and I would have sought the shelter of my cabin had I not been so overwrought with thoughts of Dr. Rushforth and Ruby Stratton.

I crossed the deck to stand by the railing. The metal bars were cold and wet with ocean spray from the ship's propellers slicing through the water. This close to the railing, the roar of the mechanics below the ship, like a steady white noise, were the only thing I could hear. The water surrounding the boat looked inky black. I thought for a moment about the creatures hiding in its depths, lurking in the ship's wake, and a chill rolled up my spine.

"You shouldn't be out here all alone," a voice slurred behind me.

I spun around, my back pressed against the cold metal railing, to find Colonel Stratton standing behind me.

"Hello, Colonel." My voice broke around his title. I hadn't even heard him walk up behind me.

He shifted his weight from side to side, and I could tell it was a struggle for him to stand. Even from ten feet away, I thought I caught a hint of alcohol on the breeze.

"It's dangerous for a woman to be out here alone," he said, stumbling over several of the words.

I wanted to tell him it was just as dangerous for a drunk man to be out on the deck alone. If he slipped and fell overboard, there was almost zero chance his body would be recovered. Once again, I thought of the sea creatures hiding in wait beneath the ship and shivered.

"I appreciate your concern, but I am very capable of taking care of myself." I smiled at him, crossing my arms over my chest to protect myself from the chill.

He took a step towards me. "Ruby was a tough girl. A real fighter."

His face screwed up as if he were going to cry, but then it smoothed out again. His glassy eyes focused on something over my shoulder.

"I'm so sorry for your loss," I said, even though I didn't think the Colonel would remember the sentiment in the morning. "Ruby didn't deserve what happened to her."

He continued staring for a few seconds, and then shrugged his shoulders, his body nearly tipping sideways from the sudden movement. "We all rather deserve death, don't we?"

I truly didn't know what to say. From a religious standpoint, it was true that all mankind deserved death, but I didn't think Colonel Stratton was looking at the situation from a religious standpoint. Besides, the man was practically saying his wife deserved to be strangled. How could anyone know how to respond to that?

I shook my head. "I don't think so."

Colonel Stratton looked into my eyes. He was still built like a walking cube—his forehead and chin were the same width, in the same way his shoulders and hips lined up, as well—but whether it was the alcohol or the trauma, something about him had softened. He looked moments from crumbling.

"I do," was all he said in return before casting his gaze back out to sea.

I took a step towards him. "Would you like me to escort you back to your room?"

He seemed unsteady and confused, and despite having thought for several days that he was a murderer—and honestly still unsure whether he hadn't killed his wife—I wanted to help him. I didn't want to wake up the next day to the news that he had gone missing, and have to spend my life knowing I could have prevented it all.

For a moment, it looked as though the Colonel would accept my offer, however, as I took another step towards him, my hand outstretched, he stumbled away from me and shook his head.

"No. No. I'll find my way back. I don't need any help." He sounded like an independent child, wanting to do everything for himself. Except, this child was drunk and twice my size.

"It's truly no trouble," I said. "Your room is next door to mine. It isn't out of my way at all."

"No!" Colonel Stratton shouted, swiping a clenched fist towards me. Even though we were still much too far apart for him to make any connection, I jumped backwards on instinct, my back reconnecting once again with the railing.

With that, the Colonel turned and walked away, his feet struggling to stay beneath his body.

Perhaps it wouldn't be such a shame if he fell overboard after all, I thought for just a second. Then, guilt set in. The man had just lost his wife to murder, and now he was trapped on the ship—the crime scene—without any idea who the murderer was. Assuming he didn't do the deed himself, of course. The least I could do was be a little forgiving.

Suddenly, the deck plunged into a darkness as deep and unknowable as the ocean below. I spun around, arms outstretched, looking for something, though I didn't know what. Something to hold onto, perhaps. Something to explain what had happened.

Electric lights dotted the exterior of the ship at night, but the one behind me had gone out. A bad bulb, perhaps? However, it seemed as if every bulb down the right side of the ship had gone out at once.

"Hello?" I called into the darkness, hoping to hear a

reassuring voice—the Captain, maybe—tell me that everything would be sorted in a matter of minutes. But there was no sound. Until I heard the footsteps.

"Hello?" This time I called out louder, more urgent, frantic. "Who's there?"

The footsteps grew closer. I could feel the vibrations move through the wooden deck and up my legs. Before I could call out again, cold hands wrapped around my throat. I tried to scream, but I couldn't force any sound out. My windpipe was being held firmly closed. I tried to inhale, but it felt as if everything below my eyes had turned to stone.

I'd always imagined that if I were being attacked, I would fight back. I'd kick and scream and fight tooth and nail for my life. In the moment when it finally happened, however, the only thing I could think was that I was dying. I could feel the life slipping from my limbs like a piece of paper fluttering in the wind. I wanted to know who was doing this and why. I wanted to fight them off. But I couldn't. It felt as though I were watching a stage play of my life, simply observing the scene, but taking no active role in it.

The darkness around me had already turned my vision black, so I didn't realize I was losing consciousness until I saw colorful spots of light in front of me like twinkling stars. In one last effort at survival, I reached up and grabbed the invisible hands that were clasped around my neck. I pulled on them, but there was no change. My brain needed oxygen desperately. The last thing I remembered was my hands slipping down the arms of my attacker, my fingers catching on something for a moment, before everything floated away, as though caught and washed out in the ocean's tide.

16

"Is she dead?"

"Oh no, another murder. My nerves can't handle another death."

"She isn't dead, she's breathing."

"But she's so pale. She looks half-dead. I won't be surprised if she's full-dead before the minute passes."

"She's moving!"

The voices came to me as though through a thick haze. I tried to wade through the fog, but my body felt heavy and far away. Did someone mention murder? Which poor soul had been taken this time?

"Her finger twitched."

"Thank the heavens."

"Rose? Rose, can you hear me?"

Did someone say my name? I could hear male and female voices, but they could have belonged to anyone. I couldn't discern whether I was familiar with any of the speakers.

"Is she unconscious?"

"No, her eyelids are fluttering. Did someone call the doctor?"

"Dr. Rushforth has been sent for."

Dr. Rushforth? I knew Dr. Rushforth. Slowly, flashes of memory lit up in my mind. Boarding the ship. Ruby Stratton's death. Mean old Lady Dixon and her niece. Mr. and Mrs. Worthing.

"Thank goodness for that."

That was Mrs. Worthing. I recognized the frantic tone of her voice now.

"Does anyone know what caused the power outage? Should we be concerned? This ship is meant to be indestructible."

Mr. Worthing, always going on about the construction of the ship.

"Honestly, dear, we have bigger things to worry about. We took Rose into our care. What will people think if she dies before first port?"

The power outage? The deck had gone dark. Yes, of course. I'd almost forgotten. The lights had flicked out all at once, and then...cold hands. My neck hurt. I hadn't felt it at first, but now my mind and my body seemed to be reconnecting. I could feel the bruises blooming just under the skin, shaped like long, thick fingers. Someone had tried to kill me.

"Did she faint?" Mrs. Worthing asked. "Perhaps the sudden darkness startled her."

"That doesn't sound much like Rose. She is a rather hearty girl," Mr. Worthing said, followed by a quick correction. "I didn't mean physically hearty, dear. Of course she is quite slim. I meant emotionally hearty."

It felt like my eyelids had been weighted down with anchors, but I fought to lift them, to see who stood around

me. I needed to know who had tried to kill me. The perpe-
trator would still be nearby, right? Or maybe not. How long
had I been lying on the deck?

"Oh, thank heavens. Rose, are you all right?"

The first face I saw was Mrs. Worthing's. She leaned
down in front of me, her hands running up and down my
arms, and then readjusting my dress so it covered my legs.

Colonel Stratton had been there on the deck with me
just before the power outage. He'd been drinking, and our
conversation had left a pit in my stomach. His warning to
me, not to be alone on the deck, had felt somewhat normal
at the time, but now I wondered whether it hadn't been
meant as a threat. He'd walked away less than a minute
before the outage. And now that I thought of it, I hadn't seen
him walk away entirely. He could have been lurking nearby,
waiting for his opportunity to strike. The power outage had
given him that, if he hadn't caused the outage himself.

"Give her a few seconds to adjust," Mr. Worthing said,
pulling his wife back.

I didn't say anything, but I was grateful. An anvil sat on
my forehead. My brain pounded against the inside of my
skull, and I began to wonder whether I should have woken
up after all. Perhaps death would have been better than the
pain I was in.

"Dr. Rushforth! Dr. Rushforth!" Mrs. Worthing began
waving the doctor down as if there was any way he could
possibly miss the large (and ever-growing) crowd of people
on the deck.

The group of people parted like the Red Sea before
Moses, and Dr. Rushforth emerged from between them,
black medical bag clutched in his fist.

"Excuse me," he said, urging aside the Worthings and a

blonde-haired woman I'd never met before who was staring at me, open-mouthed.

Dr. Rushforth was in business mode. He showed no surprise at seeing me lying on the deck; he simply placed his bag on the ground, knelt down next to it and extracted his stethoscope, and then turned to me with a small smile.

"Do you know your name?"

"Rose Beckingham," I said through a dry, aching throat. My voice sounded raspy, but I didn't know whether it was only to my own ears or whether it would be obvious to everyone standing around.

The corner of his mouth quirked up slightly, and he nodded. "Year?"

"1926."

"Do you remember me?" He looked into my eyes, and I looked back into his, wanting to prove to him that I was fine, though I felt undeniably shaky. I'd almost been murdered, but somehow, I'd survived. Or, had the murderer wished for me to live? Had it simply been a warning?

"I do," I said, nodding my head slowly, ignoring how dizzy I felt. "You are Dr. Rushforth."

The man I had, until very recently—the last few moments, in fact—wholly believed to be a murderer, I thought. Though, I decided to keep that information to myself.

He pressed the stethoscope to my chest and I took several deep breaths. He examined my head for any sign of a lump or abrasion, shined a light into my eyes, and then, for the briefest of seconds, ran his fingers across my neck.

I tensed, though I tried not to. Would he notice anything strange there? My neck felt sore, but I wouldn't know if there was any bruising until I could look in the mirror.

His eyebrow quirked up, head tilting to the side. He knew. He could tell.

"You fainted?"

I looked up at him with all the intensity I could muster and nodded. I didn't want anyone to know I'd been attacked. If Mrs. Worthing found out, she wouldn't leave me alone for the next two and a half weeks. I'd never be able to finish my investigation. And I didn't want my attacker to think they could shake me. Whoever it was, whether they stood in the crowd around me now, blending in amongst the concerned passengers, or whether they were hiding in their cabin, waiting for the news of another attack to break and send the ship into terror, I didn't want to give them the pleasure.

Dr. Rushforth looked at me for a second longer, his hand wrapping around my neck in much the same way my attacker's had, but then he nodded his head imperceptibly and rose to his feet, extending a hand down to me. I accepted it, and he pulled me to my feet.

"Miss Beckingham seems to be in perfect health," he said, turning to Mrs. Worthing, though speaking loudly enough that the whole crowd could hear him. "Just a scare from the sudden darkness."

"I'm so embarrassed," I said, looking down at the ground, trying to sell the story and hide my neck.

"You aren't the first woman to fear the dark, Rose," Dr. Rushforth said.

There was a small laugh from the crowd, and then everyone began to disperse.

"Shall I walk you back to your room, Rose?" Mrs. Worthing asked. "Mr. Worthing and I had plans on deck, but we can skip them to—"

"That won't be necessary. I don't wish to ruin your evening."

"I can escort her to her cabin," Dr. Rushforth said.

Mr. and Mrs. Worthing exchanged a glance and rather quickly agreed. I waved to them as they scurried down the deck toward whatever evening plans awaited them.

"You really don't need to walk me back. I'm feeling fine," I said, though the deck tilted slightly as I stood there. I blinked hard twice and it righted itself again.

"Someone should be there in case you...faint...again," he said, placing accusatory pauses around the word.

I nodded in agreement and looped my arm around his offered elbow. We walked in relative silence, Dr. Rushforth with his black bag, me with my arms folded tightly across my stomach. He made mention of the chilly evening, and I agreed. I commented on the evening's dinner, and he complained the potatoes had been too cold. I began to believe he wouldn't press me on why I'd fallen unconscious on the deck or why large bruises were growing across my neck. As soon as we reached the stairwell, however, he cinched his arm around my arm and leaned down to whisper in my ear.

"What really happened when the lights went out on deck? I do not believe you fainted."

"It is no concern of mine what you believe. Think as you like," I said coyly.

"Rose," he hissed. "This isn't a joke. If someone wishes you harm, someone ought to know. You could be in danger."

"You are someone," I said.

He reared back, eyes wide and wild. "What is that supposed to mean?"

"I mean, you know someone tried to harm me. That is good enough for me."

His face relaxed instantly. "The Captain should know. The investigation into Ruby Stratton's murder has stalled. If you have any idea who did this, it is only right you would share that information."

"If I had any lead into who could have killed Ruby Stratton, I would share it with the Captain immediately. Unfortunately, I know nothing more than anyone else."

This wasn't entirely true. I'd been investigating for several days, and I had a small list of suspects, which was already more information than most people had. Plus, as far away from answers as I felt, the attack on the deck only proved I was closer to solving the crime than even I knew. The murderer wouldn't bother harming me if my investigation was on the wrong course. Of course, my attack could have been entirely unrelated to Ruby Stratton's murder, but two killers on one ship? That seemed unlikely.

We reached my room, and I went to grab my key from my pocket, however, at that moment, I felt the small scrap of fabric tucked in my fist. I hadn't even realized I'd been carrying it. I quickly tried to think back to when I could have acquired it, and the only logical explanation was that I had grabbed it in my final moment of consciousness.

Dr. Rushforth looked at me curiously, his eyebrows pulled together, so I quickly shoved my fist in my pocket, releasing the fabric and grabbing the keys instead. I turned to unlock my door, doing my best to look casual.

"Thank you for the escort, Doctor. I believe I can take it from here," I said, already stepping into my cabin.

Dr. Rushforth's hand wrapped around my elbow, and before I even had time to react, he had pulled me back into the hallway and spun me around to face him. He took a step closer to me, closing the already small distance between us. His warm breath hit my skin and I nearly went cross-eyed trying to look into his face. His narrow features looked as pointed as ever, his lips puckered in disapproval.

"I know someone attempted to harm you, Rose."

"Really, Dr. Rushforth—"

He raised a hand to silence me, his other hand around my elbow clenching more tightly.

"I know someone attempted to harm you, Rose, and I will remain quiet about it for now. However," he paused, lifting his chin so he could more effectively look down his nose at me, "you should leave the investigation into Ruby Stratton's murder to someone else."

My mouth fell open slightly, shock and confusion taking up equal space in my mind. How did he know of my investigation? I hadn't told anyone.

"You are more conspicuous than you think," he said.

Aseem had said something similar to me the day I'd met him in the cargo hold. I supposed I should have assumed a grown man would suspect me of doing some amateur detective work if a twelve-year-old had been able to pick up on it. How many others knew?

"I do not wish to see you come to harm," Dr. Rushforth said. He seemed sincere, and I nodded in thanks. I didn't in any way intend to accept his advice, but it felt nice to know he cared for my safety.

"Good night, Doctor."

He stood in the hallway, watching me as I closed my cabin door, the concerned expression on his face never fading.

With the door closed and locked, I snatched the fabric from my pocket, unfurling it in my palm. It was a brown patch with three blue chevron stripes stitched into it, stacked one on top of the other.

A military patch.

I heard the cabin door next to mine open and then slam closed, and I turned to stare at the wall as though I could see through it. As though I could watch Colonel Stratton walk through the door and slip out of the dress uniform he had worn almost every day since being on the ship. Did he notice the patch from his right shoulder was missing? If not, he certainly would soon. And then what? Would he come for me again?

I stood in the middle of the room, afraid to move lest he hear me, uncertain what to do next.

17

Yet another night passed with little sleep. If the Colonel didn't kill me, exhaustion certainly would. The thought of him sleeping on the other side of the wall had been impossible to shake. As I rinsed my makeup off, I felt certain Colonel Stratton had attacked me on the deck. Who else could it have been? He'd been there only moments before, drunk, or at least acting drunk, and his wife had been murdered. The Colonel had been my main suspect from the start. He was the killer, without question.

As I climbed into bed, however, doubts began to creep in. Many men had served in the war. I'd seen more than a few men in their dress uniforms since boarding the ship. It could have been any number of them.

My opinion tossed and turned almost as much as I did throughout the night.

By the time the sun began to rise, shining through the porthole in a beam that illuminated the white room, the only thing I knew for certain was that I needed proof. I needed concrete, undeniable proof that Colonel Stratton was my attacker. Otherwise, I'd never come to a conclusion.

The bruising around my neck, which I had felt rising to the surface all night, had turned to ribbons of black and purple that wrapped around my throat like a deadly necklace. Luckily, my silk scarf seemed to cover most of the damage. I wrapped it around my neck twice, letting the ends hang on either side of my right shoulder.

Mrs. Worthing knocked on my door just as I finished adjusting the scarf in the mirror. In stark contrast to her usual lack of boundaries, she didn't barge through the door as I opened it. In fact, she stood back, looking at me as though I were a frightened animal.

"How are you feeling this morning, Rose? Any better?" she asked, her lips pouty.

I let gravity pull my mouth down, my eyes sagging with fatigue—which wasn't too far from the truth, I felt dead on my feet—though not enough to cause concern, just enough to make my excuse seem valid.

"Better, but rather shaky. I think it would be best if I spent the day resting," I said.

She nodded, eyes closed, lips pursed. "I agree entirely. You really ought to eat something, though."

My stomach growled at the mere mention of food, and I wanted some desperately, but I also didn't want to leave my cabin.

"Could you grab me a few slices of toast and a bowl of fruit from breakfast?" I asked. Giving Mrs. Worthing a task would keep her occupied and providing me with food would quell her desire to take care of me.

She brightened at the suggestion. "Absolutely. Food isn't meant to be taken out of the cafeteria, but I pity the poor crew member who tries to stop me. I'll bring up a plate directly after breakfast."

Mrs. Worthing left, and I sat on my bed, ear craned towards the wall that separated my cabin from Colonel Stratton's. All was silent for several moments, and then I heard a muffled rustling. He was still in his cabin. I lay back on the bed, arms draped over my empty stomach. The Colonel would have to leave eventually, and when he did, I'd gather my proof.

Every time a door along our corridor opened, I sat upright, praying it would be the Colonel's, but then I'd hear him moving around on the other side of the wall, and lay back again. Mrs. Worthing, true to her word, brought me four slices of toast, a kiwi, and two apples from breakfast. After she watched me begin to nibble at the monstrous amount of food, she left to attend another dance class with Mr. Worthing.

The breakfast plate lasted until lunch and a little after, sustaining me while I waited patiently—and occasionally not so patiently—for the Colonel to leave his cabin. As midday turned to late afternoon, I began to doubt whether he'd ever leave. He had to eat, right? Did he have a supply of food in his room or were crew members bringing the "grieving" widower his meals? I hadn't heard enough foot traffic next door for that to be true. Perhaps I was waiting for something that would never happen.

Then, just as doubts began to creep in, I heard it—the recognizable thud of the Colonel's door, followed by retreating footsteps.

I counted to thirty, and then opened my door. The corridor was clear. I closed my own door as carefully and quietly as possible before sneaking over to the Colonel's. Even though I had no doubt I'd heard the Colonel leave, a primal fear bloomed inside of me. What if I'd been mistaken? What if it had been some kind of a trap?

I pushed the thoughts away, trying to focus on the task at hand.

I needed to get into the Colonel's cabin, find his uniform jacket, and make sure the patch I'd been clutching in my hand after the attack belonged to him.

While waiting in my room all morning, I'd dug through my steamer trunk and pulled out a jade hairpin I'd purchased at an Indian bazaar. It had been nothing more than a beautiful curiosity to me at the time, but now with its long, sharp tip, it would function as a sort of weapon should I be attacked again. Also, the long tip conveniently functioned as a sort of lock picking device.

With another quick glance down the corridor to be sure I was alone—most everyone enjoyed the ship's many amenities in the span between lunch and dinner—I knelt down in front of the door and inserted the hairpin into the keyhole. I didn't know exactly how to pick a lock, but luckily, after only a few twists and shakes the lock clicked and I was able to push the door open. I made a mental note to always slide my own lock chain into place at night since I would no longer be able to trust the door lock alone, and then stepped into Colonel Stratton's room.

Every square inch was filled with luggage. I knew he'd moved the entirety of his cargo space into his room, but even I couldn't have imagined he would be living in such tight quarters for the remainder of the voyage. What could have been stowed amongst his luggage that he would go to such great lengths to keep it hidden? More importantly, how would I ever find his jacket in this mess? Taking a deep breath, I squelched my nerves and dug in. I didn't have any time to waste.

Several half-eaten plates of food lying on the floor near the wall lead me to believe my hunch about the Colonel having his meals delivered had been correct. I scrunched my nose at the rotten odor and pressed on towards the drawers set into the wall. I opened the first drawer and quickly closed it, having no desire to stare at or rifle through the Colonel's under garments. The second drawer contained nothing except three identical, even stacks of plain white undershirts. The third drawer was the same, except instead of shirts, it contained brown wool pants. Expecting to see the bottom drawer lined with stacks of the same button down shirts all in a row, I was surprised to find it absolutely stuffed to overflowing with a mess of satin, lace, and chiffon. In comparison to the neatly arranged other drawers, this one looked as though it had been overturned and then refilled in a hurry.

I began to sift through the contents, pulling out dresses and skirts, stockings and gloves. It looked like the entirety of Ruby's wardrobe had been confined to the one drawer. As the pile of clothes next to me began to grow nearly as tall as I was, I wondered whether I wasn't wasting my time. Unless I was investigating Ruby Stratton's fashion choices, the drawer seemed inconsequential. Then, as I removed the last blush pink satin dress from the bottom of the drawer, a small black notebook tumbled out of the folds. It looked as if it had been carefully hidden away inside the dress.

I remembered what Mrs. Worthing had said about seeing Ruby Stratton writing in a notebook on deck the first day aboard the ship. She'd been writing a letter to Mo Mo, and had hidden it away quickly to keep Mrs. Worthing from seeing the contents. Had she also managed to hide the notebook from her husband?

The first few pages were long packing lists, outlining

everything Ruby wanted to bring for the trip to England. Seeing the list, I understood why the cabin was so full of luggage and cargo. Ruby's lists were exhaustive. I flipped through a few more pages of past doodles she'd done with pencil—crude outlines of buildings and trees. Several pages later, I finally came upon what I'd been hoping to find. At the top of the page, written in loopy handwriting, were two words: Dear Mo Mo.

DEAR MO MO,

I DO NOT HAVE the slightest idea when this letter will find you—I'll mail it as soon as the ship drops anchor at the first port. I'm writing more for my own comfort than anything else. I miss talking with you. Even from a young age, you were a marvelous listener.

THE COLONEL IS TREATING me well, though he has grown curious who I spend so much time writing to. I know he worries I am writing to a young, handsome man. What a relief it would be to him to discover I am writing to a young girl, instead. (Or perhaps it wouldn't be such a comfort to him, given our circumstances.) I wish I could introduce you to him. He would adore you, as everyone does. I hope you are being treated well.

I DO NOT wish to alarm you, so please take the next few lines to be the ravings of a woman worn thin by nerves. Do your best to make the money I sent last. I know you are careful how you spend things, and I cherish you for that, but I am not sure when exactly I will be able to send more. I will sort it all out, surely, so you have nothing to worry about, but maybe you should live the next few weeks as if you do have something to worry about. If you understand my meaning. Honestly, I'm not even sure I understand my meaning. To be plain, the man from whom I had been getting money may no longer be an option.

If I decide to send this letter—I haven't decided yet whether I will rip it to shreds or not—then I hope it finds you well. Please send another photo when you have the opportunity. I dearly miss your sweet face.

All my love,
   M.

M? I flipped to the front of the notebook where Ruby had written her full name in the front flap. Why hadn't she signed her own name to the letter, or even her own initials? And she mentioned sending another photo. Did that mean the photo I'd found in the steamer trunk had been of Mo Mo? If so, Mo Mo was no more than a child, which the letter seemed to insinuate, as well. And which man had she been receiving money from? I read through the letter twice more to glean as many details as possible, and I was just deciding that I should put it away and begin my search for the jacket in earnest when I heard the handle of the cabin door jingle.

My heart froze in my chest. How long had I been reading the letter? Surely no more than a few minutes. I'd expected the Colonel to be gone longer. I quickly tried to dismiss my expectations and focus on the reality. The Colonel would walk through his door any second and I was crouched down in the corner of his cabin digging through his and his dead wife's belongings. There was only one exit, and he would be blocking it. I was doomed.

The key jiggled in the lock and the handle turned. A shaft of light poured from the crack of the door as it opened, illuminating the dim room. I clutched the Jade hairpin in my hand, point out, prepared for a fight. But then, the door stopped opening. I held my breath.

"Colonel Stratton."

I recognized the voice. The accent was unmistakable. Achilles Prideaux was in the hallway talking to the Colonel.

Fear gripped my heart, but I knew this could be my only opportunity to sneak out of the room without being detected. Even though every bone in my body wanted to stay put in the corner and await my fate, I took a step towards the door, followed by another and another. I moved until I stood just on the other side of the door from the Colonel, and I was able to peek through the crack.

The Colonel had his back to the door, having turned to face Achilles Prideaux. He was holding a silver platter, presumably with food beneath, and a glass bottle, presumably holding alcohol.

"Prideaux," Colonel Stratton responded, barking out the man's surname as though he were speaking to a soldier.

"I wanted to offer my condolences on the tragic loss of your dear wife. She was a *rose* among thorns," he said. I couldn't tell if it was my imagination or reality, but it seemed as though Monsieur Prideaux had placed a special emphasis on the word Rose.

"Thank you," Colonel Stratton said. He began to turn back towards the door, and I jumped back into the room so he would not see me observing them through the crack.

"Do you have your dinner there?" Achilles asked. "That is good that the crew is accommodating your circumstance and allowing you to eat in your room. I wish I could do the same. Dinner service can be so slow, I do wish they would *move faster*."

Once again, it seemed as though he was emphasizing certain words more than others. Did he know I was hiding in the Colonel's room? I moved to the edge of the door and peeked out again. Achilles Prideaux cast his eyes towards me for only a second, answering my question. He knew. And he was attempting to stall the Colonel for me so I could escape.

Without hesitating, I pulled the door open a bit more, just wide enough so I could slip through it. I eased myself into the hallway. I stood less than a foot behind the Colonel now, and I held my breath so it would not hit the back of his neck and alert him to my presence.

"Yes, yes," Colonel Stratton said. "I'm able to pick up my meals before the start of service."

"That's marvelous," Achilles Prideaux said. "How have you been finding the food? Sometimes ship food can be quite bland."

I tiptoed backwards towards my cabin door. I'd left it unlocked, a fact for which I was now eternally grateful, and I twisted the door knob slowly, pulling the latch from the door.

"It is fine," Colonel Stratton said, clearly ready to be back inside his cabin.

"Yes, I'm enjoying it, as well."

The conversation seemed to be stalling out as I pushed the door open as quietly as possible and stepped back into my room. I was a single second away from the relative safety of my cabin when I noticed Colonel Stratton's jacket.

It was his dress uniform—the exact jacket I'd been searching for.

I hesitated in the doorway. If I went inside, there was a good chance I wouldn't get another look at the Colonel, at least not before I was attacked again. I had to know whether he'd done it. I stepped out into the hallway and I noticed Monsieur Prideaux's eyes widening in shock and confusion. I leaned out as far as I could, hoping Colonel Stratton would not catch a glimpse of me from the corner of his eye.

"The weather has been unusually chilly, has it not?" Achilles asked.

If he was stooping to talk about the weather, I really only had a matter of seconds before the conversation died out entirely.

My entire weight was on my right foot, as I peeked around the Colonel's body, trying to get a good look at his right shoulder where I knew the patch should be. He mumbled something about the wind, and then turned towards his door, giving me a full view of his shoulder and the brown patch with blue chevron stripes. It was stitched to his jacket exactly where it had been the first time I'd seen it. Colonel Stratton could not have been my attacker.

"The wind on deck has been—" Achilles Prideaux started, trying to give me a few vital seconds to get into my cabin and shut the door, but Colonel Stratton was no longer interested in conversation.

"My food is growing cold," he said, interrupting the Frenchman before he could finish his thought.

Colonel Stratton turned, and the next few seconds passed as if in slow motion. I shifted back to my left foot, stepping inside the door of my cabin just as Colonel Stratton began to pivot towards his own cabin door. His body was turning, but unable to completely ignore social niceties, his head remained pointed towards Monsieur Prideaux, a polite smile no doubt painted on his square face. I grabbed the edge of my cabin door and began pulling it closed, turning my body so I could squeeze through the small gap. I nearly cut it too close, the door brushing against my chest and catching the delicate chiffon there, ripping it slightly. However, I still managed to squeeze inside the room and close the door behind me with a very soft thud.

I leaned against the wall and waited, breathing heavily. Had the Colonel heard anything? Had he seen me?

"Of course. I understand," Achilles Prideaux said. "Enjoy your meal."

The Colonel grunted a thank you and went into his cabin, slamming the door behind him.

I breathed for what felt like the first time all day, my lungs grabbing at the air greedily.

As soon as my breathing and my heart rate slowed to normal, I allowed myself to think on the information I'd just gathered. The Colonel had not been my attacker. But if not him, then who?

Slowly, the answer washed over me like a sunrise, soft and warm before growing to full intensity.

My attacker was likely the same person who had killed Ruby Stratton, they'd served in the military, and they knew I was growing close to solving the case. I only knew of one other person who ticked all three boxes.

Dr. Rushforth.

18

How had I not seen it? At the time of my attack, Dr. Rushforth had been my main suspect. I'd questioned him intensely that afternoon, making it clear I had my suspicions. However, as soon as he began examining me after my "fainting spell," treating me with the same level of care he'd show any of his patients, I'd dismissed him. Surely, someone so gentle and kind couldn't be a killer. Surely the hands that examined me for injuries couldn't have strangled Ruby Stratton and then wrapped themselves around my neck.

But, of course they could. And they had.

Dr. Rushforth had served in the army as a surgeon and he'd known the Strattons socially for years. I didn't yet know what cause he had to kill Ruby Stratton, but it had to have something to do with the letter she'd been writing to Mo Mo. Ruby had told me she feared for her life, and earlier that day she'd been writing to a little girl, telling her she would no longer be able to send money. That couldn't be a coincidence.

I paced around my room, ignoring Mrs. Worthing's

knocks on my door near dinnertime, allowing her to think I was asleep, and spent the evening in thought. Aside from my own suspicions and a shoulder patch, what other evidence did I have? I could tell someone I believed Dr. Rushforth to be the killer, but no one had any reason to believe me.

As I moved nervously around my room, afraid to stay put where Dr. Rushforth knew to look for me, and afraid to wander around the deck alone, lest I be attacked again, I heard a familiar rustling near the door. Unlike the first time when I'd stood back in fear, I darted across the room and stooped to pick up the piece of paper that had slid under the door.

Bottom deck, coal storage space, starboard-side.

THE WORDS WERE SCRAWLED across the page, but I knew who'd written them. I'd almost forgotten about Aseem, hiding below deck and lurking nearby, listening and observing. Perhaps that was where his strength came from, his ability to shift in and out of focus, to be front and center one moment, and on the periphery the next. I hoped he had managed to gather more information on Dr. Rushforth than I had.

I checked my makeup in the mirror, powdering over the scar on my left cheek, adjusting my scarf around the bruising on my neck, and slipped into a brown pair of t-strap heels. Before leaving, I made sure to grab the Jade hairpin and stash it in a fold of my scarf.

I earned a few curious glances from fellow passengers as

I walked down the corridors, especially as I moved to progressively lower decks. Though I had on a daytime tea dress well after dinner, I was still clearly a first-class passenger, and it was unusual for first class passengers to find themselves too far into the belly of the ship. And I was going to the very bottom.

It seemed off that Aseem would want to meet in the bottom of the ship, especially in a place where he was more likely to run into some of the ship's crew, but I figured he had his reasons. Aseem didn't seem the type to take uncalculated risks.

As I moved lower, the walls grew bare. The neutral-colored art that decorated the spaces between the first-class cabins was replaced with more doorways to smaller cabins in the lower decks. There were no sitting rooms that adjoined separate cabins into a suite, just small rooms filled with bunk beds. I tried to imagine what it would be like to share a room with a stranger, especially after a murder had been committed. I'd been nervous just sleeping alone in my cabin.

Finally, after what felt like hours, I reached the bottom deck. The lights were dimmed and the long hallway stretched on forever, the entire length of the ship. There were no portholes allowing for a glimpse outside, so the narrow hallway felt all the more oppressive. I was close enough to the propellers of the ship that I could feel the powerful thrum of them vibrating against the soles of my feet.

I was halfway down the hallway when I saw a door up ahead cracked open. The room within was dark, so I knocked softly.

"Aseem?"

I saw a shadow move inside the coal storage room. I

grabbed the door and pulled it open further, allowing enough space for me to step inside. The light from the hallway filtered inside, and I was finally able to make out the shape of the person inside. However, by the time I recognized him and tried to move away, it was too late. Dr. Rushforth plunged his hand through the door, grabbed my arm, and pulled me inside the room. He slammed the door behind him, pressing his back against it, effectively blocking my exit.

"Hello, *Rose*," he said with a snarl.

19

I wanted to scream, but I knew it would do no good. The machinery at the base of the ship let off a constant hum that dampened all other noise, like a heartbeat. Like my own heartbeat. It felt like a hummingbird had been trapped in my chest and was fighting to get out, pushing against my ribcage.

"I warned you to leave the investigation to the professionals," Dr. Rushforth said, shaking his head in disappointment. Like I was a naughty child, he the overworked parent.

"You killed Ruby Stratton." The words just needed to be said. Before whatever else happened, I needed to speak the truth, to see the investigation through to the end.

"I did," he said, nodding. "But she wasn't as sweet and innocent as she appeared."

"She did not deserve death."

"You don't know that. You don't know what she did," he said, pointing at me as he moved forward, the expression on his face deadly.

Dr. Rushforth would kill me. I could see it in his eyes, and I'd felt it in his grip that night on deck. The ease with which he'd crushed my windpipe closed said that well enough. Now, he was blocking my only path of escape and no one knew where I was. For the first time in many days, I didn't have a plan. There was no obvious next step. I needed to stall.

I quirked my head to the side. "What did she do?"

"She discovered sensitive information about my past and she used it against me."

"Blackmail?"

He nodded solemnly, as if blackmail was a reason to murder someone in cold blood.

"I wouldn't think you subject to a woman's threats," I said, in an effort to goad him into a longer explanation.

"I did not know the threats came from a woman," he said. "Certainly not a woman I dined with several times a week and whose husband was one of my dearest friends."

"What sensitive information did she have over you?"

Dr. Rushforth pulled his thin lips into an even thinner line. His feathery eyebrows came together, drawing his face into the center and giving him the appearance of a rather large rodent. It was clear he did not want to tell me.

"No need to be coy now," I said. "We both know I will not be leaving this room."

Dr. Rushforth seemed to consider my words, and then took a deep breath. "I served as a surgeon in the war.

As he began to speak, a shiver ran down my spine. Though I had already come to grips with the fact Dr. Rushforth would kill me, by launching into his admission, he had confirmed it.

"As war goes, people live and die. I am a surgeon, not a magician. One day, at the height of the fighting, three soldiers were rolled in all at once. Gaping wounds. Missing limbs. Tears. Blood. The scene was chaotic."

He waved his arms as he described the day, his eyes closing as if he were imagining it all over again.

"Nurses were using anything they could find—towels, soiled clothes, bed sheets—to sop up the blood. I was trained to operate in any kind of setting, so it didn't bother me. I did my best work that day, but within the next twenty-four hours, all three men lost their lives. There were whispers that I had lost my touch and should no longer be in an operating room, but time passed and the whispers died down and people forgot. Or, at least, I thought they had. Years later, I received an unaddressed letter in my mailbox. The writer knew about the men who died while under my care, and unless I paid a large sum of money, the writer would tell everyone how the men died."

"How *did* the men die?" I asked, unable to help myself. As scared as I was, the story was engrossing.

He shook his head, half-laughing. "It was ridiculous. Some talk of me being drunk while on duty. Absolute nonsense, of course."

"Then why did you pay them?"

He shifted his focus to me, eyes narrowed and dangerous. "Because although there wasn't an ounce of truth to the claim, I didn't want my past to come back to haunt me."

I thought of my own past, the demons lurking in my own history, and I could understand him. Except, I couldn't. Why would he spend years paying money to someone over a false claim? It didn't make any sense.

I shook my head, unable to reconcile the story he was telling with the reality of the situation. "You could have gone to the police or to your employer. If the claims were false, surely you could have—"

He shouted loudly, running his hands through his hair. "Fine. You are right. You will be dead soon, anyway. No need to keep up the lie. I was drunk. The day had been a slow one, and I'd partaken in a few too many gin and tonics. When the soldiers arrived in bloody tatters, it was clear I was the only surgeon in the building with enough experience to save them. Had I been sober, I believe I would have. Unfortunately, I cut a few corners, made a few mistakes, and the men lost their lives. Somehow, Ruby Stratton discovered my secret, and she used it to take advantage of me."

He exhaled loudly, as though he had sat down a heavy load after years of carrying it. He looked up at me and smiled. "What a relief. It feels good for someone to know the truth."

"How did you discover Ruby Stratton was your blackmailer?"

He raised a finger in the air to let me know I'd made an interesting point. "That was pure luck. Because I considered her a friend, I happened to tell her that because of a few misplaced bets, I was running low on cash. Then, for the first time in months, I didn't receive any correspondence from my blackmailer at the first of the month. A few weeks later, Ruby asked about my financial situation and I told her I had settled all of my debts. Days later, even though it was only the middle of the month, a letter arrived in my mailbox. I put two and two together."

"Why would Ruby be blackmailing you?" I asked. "What would she do with the money?"

"You actually came close to solving that piece of the puzzle," Dr. Rushforth said, clapping his hands together a few times in congratulation. "The 'Mo Mo' your Mrs. Worthing saw Ruby writing to? That was the pet name Ruby gave to her daughter."

Daughter? I didn't know Ruby had a daughter. The girl in the photograph from the steamer trunk looked nearly ten-years-old. Ruby had to have been pregnant when she was only around fifteen, surely many years before she met the Colonel.

"Ruby's child was illegitimate, and a complete secret from her husband. The sad thing is, I would have taken pity on the poor woman had she told me of her circumstances. I may have even offered up some money to buy the child a winter coat or some new dresses. But instead, Ruby manipulated me. She chose her path," he said with a snarl.

"The girl was a secret. If Ruby had confessed, she could have lost her husband, her life. She would have had no way to provide for her child."

Dr. Rushforth didn't seem to hear me. He looked over my shoulder, his eyes fixed on a point in his memory, and a smile slipped across his lips. "I stood with the Strattons while our luggage was being loaded onto the ship. Ruby was smiling, tucking a strand of dark hair behind her ear when I leaned down and whispered: 'Mo Mo.' She practically fainted with fright. After killing her, I'd planned to throw her body overboard. People occasionally fall overboard on ships. Bodies are never recovered. It happens. However, I was interrupted before I could dispose of her body. I tried to take care of it in the morning, but Lady Dixon and Jane were out for their morning walk."

Dr. Rushforth shook his head in disappointment and then looked over as though he'd almost forgotten I was there. "You are one to talk about secrets. You know all about secrets, don't you *Rose Beckingham*?"

I narrowed my eyes at him. "What do you mean?"

"I mean," he said, taking a step towards me, forcing me into the corner of the small room. "You are a top of the line impersonator. Truly, world class. However, your accent needs some work."

I tried to say something, but it felt like I'd swallowed my tongue. "I don't know what—"

"I've spent time in America. I know what an American accent sounds like. When you are flustered, your British accent falters and your real voice slips out. I doubt most people notice, but I picked up on it. I do not know who you truly are, but there is one thing I know for certain. You are not the English-born, highly educated heiress to the Beckingham family fortune."

I understood what Dr. Rushforth meant now about it feeling good for someone to know the truth. For weeks I'd been faking the accent and the family connections, doing my best to blend in and talk as little about the car explosion as possible. Now, however, finally, I could tell my story.

"You shared your story with me, so it only feels fair I should share mine with you," I said, dropping the British accent for the first time, allowing my native New York dialect to shine through. It felt like taking off a heavy hat after a long day.

Dr. Rushforth tipped his head to me, waving his hand for me to continue.

"My name is Nellie Dennet. I was Miss Rose Beckingham's companion while she lived in India, however, as you have already surmised, I was born in America. I grew up in the Five Points district of New York. If you know anything at all about the city, you'll know that area is a slum. Crime-infested, disease-ridden, over populated. My childhood held many horrors, one of which—I won't bore you with the details—left me alone in the world at the age of fourteen. I spent a few months in an orphanage before a wealthy patron of the orphanage took me in, employed me, educated me, and found me the position in the Beckingham household. I was sent out to the Beckingham's in

India and stayed in their home for many happy years, straddling the line between a dear friend and a maid to their daughter Rose. We looked a lot alike, Rose and I. While still young, we enjoyed fooling strangers into mistaking us for one another. Rose learned to imitate my New York accent, and I mastered her British one. Or, I suppose, *nearly* mastered it."

I remembered Rose's curly blonde hair, the day we'd cut it into a fashionable bob, nearly sending her mother into a conniption. Then the image shifted. I saw her pale, lifeless, covered in soot and debris. The explosion had sent her flying towards the opposite side of the car, but as the smoke cleared, I saw her hand, fingers curled and bloody next to me.

"I was in the car with Rose and her parents in Simla. A violent revolutionary lobbed the explosive through the driver's side window, and the entire Beckingham family, the people I'd called my own family for ten years, were gone. Rose's face was burned beyond recognition, but somehow I escaped with little more than a scar. When I woke up in the hospital, I realized the mistake my rescuers had made. They'd assumed me to be Rose. I didn't plan to impersonate her, but then I began to wonder what Rose would want for me. Would she want me to be alone in the world again? Would she want me to be penniless and homeless? Or, would she want me to have the life that would have been hers? I decided to assume the role and my new life. The Worthings had seen photos of Rose but they hadn't met her, so they didn't possess a single doubt that I was precisely who I claimed to be. I knew I would miss being Nellie Dennet, but becoming Rose had one major advantage."

Dr. Rushforth chuckled to himself. "I assume that advantage includes the large Beckingham inheritance that

Rose would claim once back in England? She was an only child, was she not?" he asked.

I shook my head. "I have no interest in money for its own sake. I made it far enough in my life without it. But assuming the identity and inheritance of Rose gives me the...freedom...to complete a personal mission. To right a wrong from my past."

"What wrong might that be?" Dr. Rushforth asked.

I shook my head. "A killer like you would never understand my full plan."

Dr. Rushforth shrugged, and I sensed the time for sharing was over. I didn't know how long I'd been in the coal storage room, but it felt long enough that Mrs. Worthing would have noticed me missing from my room. Were people looking for me? Was anyone concerned?

"Why have you told me all of this, Rose? Or, Nellie, should I say?"

"For the same reason you've confessed your crime to me. We both know only one of us is leaving this room alive, and the one left behind will have no further need of secrets," I said.

My words must have spurred Dr. Rushforth into action because he suddenly lunged across the small room, hands extended for my throat. I ducked, causing his hands to smash into the wall behind me, and made a beeline beneath his arm. I nearly grabbed the door handle, but before I could, Dr. Rushforth's thick arm wrapped around my waist and pulled me back, slamming me onto the floor.

"I never wanted to harm you," Dr. Rushforth panted. "If you'd stayed out of my business, I would have let you move through life with your false accent and identity. I wouldn't have said anything, but now you've left me no choice."

The Doctor reached into his jacket and pulled something out. He held it in front of his face, and even in the dimness, I could see the outline of the pistol in his hands. He was going to shoot me.

My arms were pinned down by one of Dr. Rushforth's arms, but thinking quickly, I kicked out with my leg, connecting with his wrist and sending the gun clattering across the floor. In the scramble to retrieve it, Dr. Rushforth released my arms, allowing me to pull the jade hairpin from the folds of my scarf. He leaned across me, arm outstretched towards the gun, and I wasted no time plunging the pin into his side. Blood immediately stained the white fabric of his shirt, and he howled in pain, rolling onto the floor, a hand pressed to his wound.

I kicked out at him again, this time landing a blow to his nose. He rolled away from me, trying to place a safe distance between himself and my flailing limbs. I stood up, the pin held in my outstretched hand as a warning, trying to keep him from charging at me again.

Dr. Rushforth still blocked the door with his body, so my chances at escape were slim unless I could kill him. Only, I did not want to. I would, absolutely. Especially if he charged at me again. But I had no desire within me to kill the angry man before me.

Then, over the humming of the propellers, I heard a single shout. I couldn't tell what the voice said, but I heard it. And by the way Dr. Rushforth turned his head, I knew he heard it, too.

The voice sounded again, this time closer. "Rose!"

Without hesitation, I screamed back. "In here! Help, I'm in—"

Dr. Rushforth lunged for me, trying to keep me from shouting. As his hands grabbed at my collarbone, I forced the hairpin into the dense flesh of his shoulder. He shouted and fell to the floor in a heap. Knowing I likely wouldn't have another opportunity, I made a beeline for the door and ripped it open, practically throwing myself into the hallway and directly into the arms of Achilles Prideaux.

"Are you hurt, Rose?" he asked, his eyes concerned but frantic, searching around for my attacker.

I opened my mouth to answer, and then stopped, reminding myself who I was supposed to be. I was Rose Beckingham.

"I'm all right," I said, the accent coming out strained. I'd been doing the British accent for nearly a month, but just five minutes with my regular voice, and I was already finding the adjustment difficult. "Dr. Rushforth is still in the room. He killed Ruby and he tried to kill me."

Monsieur Prideaux lifted his walking stick in front of him, and with a quick flash of his wrist, a thin, sharp blade protruded from the end. He tightened his grip on the stick and moved towards the door. Before he could make it to the door, though, Dr. Rushforth burst from the room. He had retrieved the gun and was pointing it at Achilles.

"Stand back," he shouted. "Do not move or I will shoot."

"Do you intend to kill us both?" Achilles asked. His voice was even and professional. Even though Dr. Rushforth had the gun, it felt as though Achilles held the power.

"If necessary."

"What story will you tell, then?" Achilles asked. "How will you explain our deaths?"

"A crazed murderer. A murder-suicide. I will find a reasonable explanation."

"There is no reason in any of this," I said, taking a step towards Dr. Rushforth, trying to place myself between the gun and Achilles Prideaux. I didn't want to see an innocent man shot and killed because he had been trying to save me.

Dr. Rushforth opened his mouth to speak, but voices echoed down the hallway, distracting him. Monsieur Prideaux and I turned to see Captain Croft, the Worthings, and a mess of crew members running down the hallway towards us.

"There's no way out," I said, turning back to Dr. Rushforth. "Put down the gun and give yourself up."

Dr. Rushforth looked from my face to the people moving towards him down the hallway. His eyes were wide, face pale. Then, unbelievably, he looked back at me and smiled.

"My dear, there is always a way out."

Then, he lifted the pistol to his temple, closed his eyes, and pulled the trigger.

20

Mrs. Worthing did not leave my room all night. She slept on the floor next to my bed in a pile of spare blankets, though I tried several times to convince her to go back to her own bed.

"You've been through a trauma, dear. I can't leave you when you need me most," she said, her eyes brimming with tears.

I stopped pressing the issue when I began to realize that, perhaps, Mrs. Worthing needed me slightly more than I needed her.

Though Dr. Rushforth had killed himself less than four feet from me, everyone in the hallway had seen it. The spectacle was not one that could be easily ignored. The blood. The smell of gun powder. The sound. It had taken me back to Simla, to the explosion that started it all. I had a basis for how to handle such gory sights. I locked them away in the back of my mind, thinking on them as little as possible. Mrs. Worthing, however, had no such coping mechanism. If sleeping on the floor next to me helped her in any way, I would not be the person to discourage her.

I knew we were set to dock briefly in Aden the next morning, so I woke up earlier than usual, sleep having evaded me most of the night anyway. Mrs. Worthing, however, seemed to have been thoroughly exhausted by the previous day's excitement. She slept on her nest of blankets, mouth open and snoring while I slipped into a long white skirt, black-toed oxford heels, and a pink sweater. I did not bother to hide the green and purple bruises around my neck or the scar on my cheek. If everyone on the ship hadn't yet become familiar with the tale of how I discovered Dr. Rushforth was the killer, they would know by breakfast. So, there was no sense in trying to blend into the crowd any longer. I slipped from the room quietly, managing not to wake Mrs. Worthing.

I spotted Lady Dixon and Jane on their morning walk, and surprisingly, Lady Dixon stopped to speak with me.

"I hear Dr. Rushforth was the killer," she said, her voice fluctuating between a question and a statement.

I nodded. "Unfortunately, yes."

She pursed her lips. "I never liked the man."

If I'd learned anything in the previous week, it was that it was much easier to simply agree with Lady Dixon than to argue. As I nodded in blind agreement, I noticed a large brooch hanging from the side of her purse.

"Did you find your brooch?" I asked.

She looked down at her bag, a smile spreading across her face. "Yes, Jane found it last night. It had been in our room the entire time."

I peeked around Lady Dixon to see Jane standing a little taller behind her. "I'm sure Lady Dixon is quite grateful to you, Jane. With as much searching as the two of you did, it is a wonder it was in your cabin all along."

Lady Dixon patted the brooch with three fingers and

then smiled up at me. "A wonder, indeed, but I am beyond glad to have it back in my possession. It is one of the few things I have left of my mother's."

Jane's smile faltered ever so slightly, and when I raised an eyebrow in her direction, her cheeks flamed, though her eyes never left mine. I could see her pleading with me not to voice my suspicion aloud, and I winked at her. Her secret would be safe with me. It was a clever plan, after all. Lady Dixon loved the brooch more than anything, and she would certainly cherish the person who found it for her. She did not need to know the person who found it had also been the person to take it.

I left the two women to finish their walk, and wove my own path around the deck, through the dining room, and into the small café that was just opening for the day. I looked at the table where I'd sat with Dr. Rushforth the morning of Ruby's murder. A chill ran down my spine when I realized how coolly he'd behaved, especially after having killed someone only hours before. I tried to push thoughts of him away, but I suspected it would be a long time before I went a day without thinking of Dr. Rushforth. On the bright side, however, with Dr. Rushforth's suicide, the secret of my true identity was safe—for now.

I took up residence in a wicker chair at the bow of the ship, watching as we neared port.

As soon as the ship dropped anchor, two white boxes, roughly human-shaped were brought up from below deck and moved off the ship. And then local police flooded the promenade. Even though I'd given my full statement to Captain Croft, explaining everything I knew, the police still made a beeline for me. I repeated my story to several offi-cers, but by the time the third officer came to question me, Achilles Prideaux—once again arriving to save me in the nick of time—stepped in. He spoke to the police in low tones, using a language I did not know. I had no idea what he said, but the officers seemed satisfied with his explana-tion and left.

"Thank you once again, Monsieur," I said, rising from my chair for the first time in hours.

Achilles tapped his walking stick on the wooden deck once and smiled. "Do not mention it. Though, I must warn you, I will be disembarking here in Aden before continuing on to England on a later vessel. So, I will not be around should you require my assistance again."

"Why are you stopping here?" I asked.

He shrugged. "Business calls."

"Then, I suppose this is goodbye, Monsieur."

"Only if you wish it to be." Achilles Prideaux reached around to his back pocket and pulled out a small white card, handing it to me.

The card simply said his name and provided an address and telephone number. Achilles pointed to the address on the card. "Call on me at my home in London should you ever find yourself in need of my services."

He turned on his heel and began walking towards the gangplank.

"Oh, Monsieur Prideaux," I called after him.

He stopped and looked over his shoulder at me.

"How did you know where to find me last night?" I asked. The question had kept me up most of the night.

"A small Indian boy tipped me off." He smiled and then was gone.

After he left, it occurred to me that I had no idea exactly

what services Achilles Prideaux provided. Later that day, I asked a middle-aged crew member whether he had any knowledge of Achilles Prideaux.

"The famous detective?" he asked.

I tilted my head at him in confusion.

"I'm almost certain that is who you mean. He just disembarked this morning to smooth over the matter of the murder with the local authorities."

I thanked the man for his information and fingered the business card in my coat pocket.

I'd spent the last week playing detective while a real detective had been living just across the hall. What insights he could have provided. I now wondered whether, much like Dr. Rushforth, Achilles Prideaux didn't have some inkling that perhaps I wasn't all I claimed to be. Surely that was what he had meant on our first meeting when he had spoken of my keeping a dangerous secret. He could not guess exactly what that secret was, but he had obviously sensed I was playing some sort of dangerous game.

For most of the ship's voyage, I'd wished to never see him again. But now, suddenly, I found myself rather hoping our paths would once again cross.

THE NEXT TWO weeks of the voyage passed much more peaceably than the first. After Aden, we passed through the Suez Canal and continued on to the ports of Said, Malta, Marseilles, and Gibraltar, before crossing the stormy Bay of Biscay.

On one of the last days of the trip, the sun was just beginning to set, the sky a wash of blues and oranges, and I found myself standing at the bow of the ship. The English coast was a thick strip on the horizon. I knew in less than a day, I would be at Southampton, the last port before London. Soon I would be standing on English soil.

In London, Mr. and Mrs. Worthing, who I had grown rather fond of, would release me into the care of the remaining Beckingham family. None of the waiting Beckingham relations had seen the real Rose since childhood so, with a little luck, I might just pull off my continued pretense. After that, my new life would officially begin. The thought sent a flutter through my stomach.

A small cough came from behind me, and I spun just in time to see Aseem wave to me from the door to the decks below. I hadn't seen him since our meeting in the maintenance closet, but I knew he was responsible for sending Achilles Prideaux to save me. I smiled at him warmly and waved in return. He disappeared below the deck, and I hoped he would manage to escape the ship when it docked at its final destination. The thought of what would become of such a young boy alone on the London streets left me feeling sick. But if any child could take care of himself, it was Aseem. He seemed incredibly capable.

I turned back to the horizon. Even though I had looked away for only a few seconds, the sky already seemed darker. The blue had faded to a deep Indigo, the same shade as the ocean.

Despite the distraction brought on by the murder of Ruby Stratton and the death of Dr. Rushforth, I knew true danger still lay ahead. I had to maintain my false identity as Rose in order to fool the rich Beckingham relations who would be anxiously awaiting my return in London. Claiming the inheritance meant for Rose was the only hope I had of completing a secret, personal mission I had put off for too many years.

I reached for the thin chain that always hung around my neck, pulling the locket free of my dress. I'd taken out the small note folded inside enough times to know the messy scrawl of the message by heart: *Help me.*

I squeezed the locket and then replaced it beneath the protective layer of my clothes.

"Hold on a little longer," I whispered into the sea wind. "I'm coming."

~

Continue following the mysterious adventures of Rose Beckingham in
"A Grave Welcome."

EXCERPT

FROM "A GRAVE WELCOME: A ROSE BECKINGHAM MURDER
MYSTERY, BOOK 2."

Stepping off the gangplank and touching solid ground for
the first time in three weeks, I felt as though I was discovering a new continent. I was Magellan finding the East
Indies, Roald Amundsen landing at the North Pole. Of
course, London had been long discovered before the likes of
Rose Beckingham set foot there, but that thought didn't
dampen my excitement. I had arrived.

I looked back up at the hulking mass of the ship behind
me. The *RMS Star of India* had borne me over rough seas,
both figuratively and literally, and I was grateful to her for
bearing the journey so well.

"Watch it!"

A woman carting a steamer trunk and two rambunctious
children plowed into my shoulder, nearly knocking me
back. I stopped to straighten myself, adjusting the brim of
my beige cloche hat over my curls and smoothing out the
travel creases in my tea gown. The dress had felt perfectly
adequate for the weather in India, but the air in London had
a chill to it. The wind bit against my exposed skin.

"Is there no better place for you to stand?"

A man with a twirled mustache stood only a few feet away with his arms full of luggage, sneering down at me so I wouldn't be able to miss the fact that I was directly in his path and being an utter nuisance. My cheeks flamed with embarrassment and I scrambled to get out of his way and away from the passengers disembarking the ship. Everyone had seemed so carefree while we were at sea—even with a murder investigation ongoing for most of the voyage—but now everyone looked harried. They scurried away from the ship and into the maze of the city like each one was already late for a meeting.

I turned on my heel, spinning in a full circle in search of Mr. and Mrs. Worthing, the couple who had acted as my chaperones for the duration of the voyage from Bombay to London. In all honesty, they had done little in the way of protecting me. Under their care, I still managed to unknowingly befriend a murderer and nearly be murdered by the same man. However, I couldn't blame them for that. I chose to dive head first into the investigation of who had killed Ruby Stratton, which placed me in a considerable amount of danger. In fact, the majority of the ship's passage had been spent trying to get away from the Worthings so I could investigate. But even still, I wanted to bid them farewell. I needed to thank them for their kindness and generosity.

As more and more passengers continued to move down the gangplank and fill the area surrounding the dock, it became more unlikely I would find the Worthings. Surely, they hadn't left without seeing me one last time? Mrs. Worthing had pulled me in for a cursory hug on our way out of the cabin, and Mr. Worthing had hurried her along, insistent on the fact we would have time to say goodbye once we were on land. But now, they were nowhere to be found.

Pulling my modest steamer trunk along behind me, I weaved my way through the crowd of people reuniting with family members and asking for directions towards their destination in the city. The crush of people didn't feel unfamiliar. The noisy, crowded streets of Bombay had prepared me for that. However, the pale faces were striking. Everything about London—based on the little I'd seen so far—seemed pale in comparison to India. The sky was a thick gray color, hanging over the stone city like fleece. Where India had been golden sunshine and red dirt and tanned skin, London was faded and foggy and cold. A pang of sudden homesickness sprung up in my chest for the warm and vivacious country I would likely never see again.

I shook my head and tried to look at the city with new eyes. I couldn't wander around London in awe and wonder. I was supposed to have been here before. More than that, I had to create the illusion that I'd *lived* in London before. The slate gray city should feel like coming home. I closed my eyes and tried to channel the other Rose's enthusiasm for the place. All the time I knew her in India, she told me repeatedly how much she missed London.

"You would love the shopping there," she said one day while we sat on her bed, fanning ourselves from the heat of the Indian summer. "Custom-made hats and dresses in any fabric you could imagine."

"You can find custom-made hats and dresses in Bombay," I countered, fingering the hem of my bright yellow sun dress.

Rose fell back on the bed, her blankets nearly swallowing her up. "It's not the same. London is where fashion lives and breathes, Nellie. By the time the latest fashions arrive here, everyone in London is on to something new. I can't wait to get home."

The memory fell upon me like a stone, crushing the breath out of me. In that moment it was hard to believe Rose could be dead. A tear fell from the corner of my eye, and I swiped at it with my gloved hand, dabbing away the moisture so as not to smudge my makeup. I had assumed Rose's identity five weeks ago, yet I still felt entirely inadequate. I didn't have her dramatic flair, and I worried everyone could see that. Of course, having supposedly survived what had killed her parents, Rose would have good reason to seem less enthusiastic now.

Lost in thought, I'd wandered across the street from the ship and down a narrow side street. Mrs. Worthing would have opted for the least busy passage into the city, so I knew I had a better chance of finding her and her husband there than on the main roads. Still, the stream of cars and passengers coming away from the docks filled the street and the sidewalks. I was a helpless fish caught in the current. I swiveled my head, standing on my toes to try and see above the crush of the crowd, but finally, I sunk down onto my feet and let myself be washed away.

Eventually, I came to a wide bridge where I was able to duck out of the walkway and stand in the shade of the arch. Since the day had already been gray and overcast, the underside of the bridge was nothing but inky shadows. An alley ran alongside the structure and it looked to cross behind a row of buildings and open onto another busy street that ran down to where the ship had docked. Perhaps the Worthings had gone down a busy street in search of me just as I had gone down a vacant street in search of them.

I could see more people with luggage, clearly having come from the ship, up ahead, but I also saw regular Londoners. People going about their daily commute. Men loading cargo ships, boys waving rags and shouting their price for a shoe shine. The constant din of voices and cars whirred around me like a machine and I thought how easy it would be to get lost in such a large city. Then, a voice cut through the noise, closer than the others.

A man stood in the shadow of a low, stone building, his back to me. He wore a dark coat and a fashionable fedora hat. His arms were waving animatedly and the wind carried his voice my way. He was angry, that much was clear.

I took another step forward and a second man appeared just behind the corner. He was shorter than the other man, his face indistinct in the darkness, nothing but hard lines and blotchy cheeks. He had a thick mess of dark hair on top of his head that he tried to hide under a dark gray flat cap.

"You're angry for nothing, Frederick," the one in the flat cap said. "I didn't do anything wrong."

I could hear a scowl in the other man's voice. "What kind of fool do you take me for? I saw the two of you cozied up together."

"Your imagination is very vivid, then, because no such thing happened."

The man in the fedora lunged out at the other, pushing him hard in the chest so that he stumbled backward.

I jumped at the suddenness of the attack, falling back into the stone arch of the bridge, catching myself with the palms of my hands. A jagged rock scraped the back of my neck as I fell and I winced at the sharp pain.

Then, the shouting stopped. The voices that had, only a moment before, been reaching a crescendo, had gone completely quiet. I pressed myself against the bridge, hoping they wouldn't see me. Why hadn't I stayed near the ship? I'd been in London for a matter of minutes and already I'd found myself in a deserted alley in the company of two angry men.

I counted to thirty and held in my sigh of relief when the voices resumed.

"You don't want a quarrel with me. It will not end well for you."

I couldn't see who had offered that ominous warning as I was already halfway down the alley, headed in the direction I'd originally come from, towards the protection of the crowded street.

Stepping back onto the crowded street felt like experiencing daylight for the first time after a month of darkness. The weather, which had only moments before felt cold and gloomy, suddenly warmed my cool skin.

It felt as though everyone I passed knew where I'd just been. I took deep breaths, trying to calm my rapidly beating heart. As it always did during times of stress, my hand reached for the locket around my neck. The locket I'd kept pressed against my heart for years, carrying it with me always. Except, for the first time since I could remember, I grabbed at empty air. Forgetting all decency, I pulled at the collar of my dress and looked down my front, but the inside of my gown was empty. Still, my fingers reached for the clasp at the back of my neck. Once again, there was nothing. I'd lost it.

My feet stopped moving. I stood frozen on the street, disregarding the shouts of the crowd around me, people hurrying through their lives, ignoring my heartbreak. How had I lost it? When?

Then came the memory of jumping back into the stone. The sharp pain at the back of my neck. I'd lost it in the alley. Immediately, I turned on my heel to make my way back to the alley, all fear of the fighting men lost to my determination to once again have my locket safely around my neck.

"Rose, dear!"

Mrs. Worthing was waving a handkerchief above her head as she walked down the sidewalk towards me, Mr. Worthing trailing behind. Her lips were pursed together, her cheeks red from the wind.

"Where did you wander off to once we disembarked the ship?" she asked, pulling me briefly into her arms for a hug. She did not wait for me to answer. "I know you are a grown woman and not actually in need of our guidance, but we swore to see you safely to London and our job is not complete until you are happily in the company of your relatives."

Mr. Worthing walked ahead of us, talking over his shoulder as he went. "We need to get back to the passenger entry office. Last night I put a call through to your uncle, Rose. Lord Ashton seems to be a fine man. Fine man. He said there would be a car waiting for you at the port's entry office once you left the ship."

I wanted to turn back and find my locket. I wanted to forget about the London branch of the Beckingham family and the Worthings and search for the necklace, but I couldn't. The locket's importance was wrapped up in my own personal mission, and without spilling all of my secrets, no one would understand why it meant so much to me. Without the Beckinghams and the Worthings believing my story entirely, I wouldn't be able to help anyone. Assuming Rose's identity and coming to London would be for nothing. So, for the sake of my ultimate goal, I followed the Worthings back towards the ship.

"There is no need to be nervous, Rose," Mrs. Worthing said, squeezing my elbow. "Your family will be so pleased to see you. I'm sure they've been beside themselves with grief and worry."

It was then I decided it wouldn't do any harm to tell the Worthings what I'd seen. Mr. Worthing could notify a police officer and they could be told where they might return my locket should it be found by any passersby.

"Oh, I am not nervous about seeing the Beckinghams again," I said, though this was nothing close to the truth. I was terrified of meeting Rose's relations, considering it would be for the first time, even though I was meant to have known them my whole life. "I did not plan to mention it, but I can't push the thought from my mind a second longer. Moments before you found me on the road behind us, I had just run away from a rather disturbing encounter."

"Run away?" Mrs. Worthing asked, no doubt thinking of how unladylike I had looked while doing it.

"Disturbing encounter?" Mr. Worthing echoed, concern etched in the lines of his face.

I turned to him and nodded solemnly. "Yes, I believe I witnessed an attempted robbery of some kind. Two men were shouting at one another in an alley and one man lunged at the other. Fearing for my own safety, I ran from the scene and did not see the outcome, but it looked like a violent altercation."

Mrs. Worthing pressed a gloved hand to her open mouth. "Good heavens! Are you hurt?"

I reached for her hands and held them in my own, squeezing her fingers in a reassuring manner. "No, Mrs. Worthing. I am perfectly safe. Excepting a gold locket I dropped in the excitement, I am perfectly well."

"Did you get a good view of either of the men?" Mr. Worthing asked, standing on the tips of his feet, trying to see above the crowd, as if he thought the men I spoke of might be creeping up on us. "We should probably report what you saw, before those fellows can do any harm."

No sooner had he said the words than Mrs. Worthing reached her hand into the flow of traffic around us and pulled a passing police officer out by his elbow as though she were drawing a fish from a river barehanded. "Sir, we have a crime to report."

The officer, a young man with pale hair and an even paler face, straightened his hat upon his head and stared at the Worthings, a look of bewilderment spread across his face. Then he looked over at me, and his expression softened. His eyes turned up in surprise and his lips fell apart. A blush crept into his cheeks.

"What seems to be the trouble?" he asked, not taking his eyes from me.

"Tell him what you saw, Rose." Mrs. Worthing shifted from one foot to the other, trying to gain the attention of the officer, but he kept his gaze fixed on me. "She encountered a violent altercation nearby. Two men."

The officer looked from me to Mrs. Worthing and back again. "Is this true?"

I nodded, my hand moving absentmindedly to my cheek. I felt the lightly scarred skin over my dented cheekbone, and turned away from him. "Yes, it's true. The men were two streets back in an alley."

The officer looked over my head and diagonally, as if he could see through buildings and locate the men without taking another step. After a few seconds, he tipped his hat and smiled at me. "I'll look into it."

"Thank you," I said, having forgotten the reason I'd told the Worthings about the altercation at all. Luckily, Mrs. Worthing couldn't be so easily distracted by a smooth, handsome face.

"Rose also lost a locket near the scene. If you discover it, have it returned to Miss Rose Beckingham at the home of Lord and Lady Ashton," she said, emphasizing the names of my aunt and uncle clearly.

His eyebrows rose in recognition and with one final smile and nod of his hat, the officer cut a path down the road, headed for the scene.

By the time we reached the ship again, the crowd around the dock had thinned. It was no surprise everyone had cleared out quickly. The wind off the ocean was icy and sharp, slicing through my clothes and giving me chills. Luckily, the passenger entry office had plush chairs and a fire roaring in the hearth while we waited for the car. I couldn't remember ever seeing a fireplace in use while in India.

"I'm going to be sad to see you go, Rose" Mrs. Worthing said, dabbing at her dry eyes with a handkerchief.

I didn't doubt her sincerity. On the contrary, in the weeks I'd come to know Mrs. Worthing, I knew she had a very large heart and rarely said anything she didn't mean entirely. However, she also had a flare for the dramatic. Mopping up her pretend tears simply made the moment more memorable, which was why she'd done it.

"We will see her again, dear," Mr. Worthing said, patting his wife's shoulder and looking over her head to find me and offer a reassuring smile. "Just because our voyage is ending does not mean our friendship must. We will all be living in the same city, after all."

I nodded in agreement. "Yes, absolutely. I won't allow us to never see one another again."

"You'll come for dinner, then?" Mrs. Worthing asked, her voice full of hope.

"Only if you promise to dine with me once I'm settled into my own home," I said.

"You won't live with the Beckinghams?" Mrs. Worthing asked. "I assumed you would want to live with family for the time being."

I shrugged. "I suppose only time will tell. Perhaps I will decide I enjoy the Beckinghams and test their good faith."

Mrs. Worthing pulled me in for another hug and pressed her lips against my hair. "I have cherished our time together these last few weeks. It would take someone of very little good faith to tire of you."

"A car has arrived," Mr. Worthing said, breaking up the emotional hug to point to the curb just in front of the office. I turned towards the window and away from Mrs. Worthing just in the nick of time. I was moments away from shedding very real tears. I had so few people in the world who cared about me. It made me happy to think I could add the Worthings to that list. Of course, they believed me to be Rose Beckingham, daughter of a deceased British government official in India, but that seemed like an unnecessary detail.

"Oh, this is all happening so quickly," Mrs. Worthing said, wringing her hands. "Do you have everything you need, Rose?"

I looked down at my small steamer trunk. It was the only thing I'd taken with me when we left India. After the attack that killed the true Rose Beckingham and her parents, it had been too dangerous for me to go back to the house where they had lived for so many years, for fear of another attack. I'd bought what I needed before leaving India with the promise that I would receive my inheritance from my family back in London and have plenty of money to replace what-ever possessions I wished.

"I believe so," I said.

Mrs. Worthing nodded her head and glanced around the small room, double-checking that was true. Then, she stood in front of me and placed her hands on my shoulders. "You are a brave young woman, Rose Beckingham. I can't begin to imagine the horrors you've experienced these last few weeks. I only hope your future is much brighter than your recent past."

Once again, tears welled behind my eyes and I swallowed them back, my throat thick. "Thank you, Mrs. Worthing."

Mr. Worthing patted my back quickly, and I glanced up at him to see a slight mist in his eyes, though he was clearly trying to ignore it. "Well. Enough with the goodbyes. We will see one another again. We need to get you to the car before the driver leaves you behind."

He took my trunk and pushed on my lower back, leading me towards the door. Suddenly, a nervous ball of energy grew in my chest. The next phase of my plan was beginning, and I wasn't as confident as I'd been at the start. Fooling the Worthings into believing I was Rose Beckingham had been easy. They hadn't known Rose and had only seen her in old photographs. Rose's relations, however, would have a much better memory of her features and habits. They had shared a family history with Rose that I was not a part of. Would I be able to fake my way through old memories and familial anecdotes?

As we stepped onto the sidewalk, a chauffeur slid from the driver's seat and moved to meet us at the front of the car, his hands behind his back. He wore a dark gray jacket with two rows of buttons cutting vertically down the front, paired with matching pants, and a high pair of black boots. He had a gray cap pushed back on his head, framing his tanned cheekbones and wavy auburn hair.

"Miss Rose?" he asked, already bending his upper body in a low bow without awaiting confirmation. "I'm sorry to be late. I had a bit of trouble finding where I was meant to park."

The man seemed full of nervous energy. His hands folded and unfolded behind his back and his eyes darted from me to the Worthings continuously, as if unable to rest on any one face for too long. I wondered whether his anxiety came from fear of disappointing me or his employers. I hoped it was the former. I wanted the Beckinghams to be abundantly kind people. The sort of people who would be much too afraid of offending anyone to ask whether they were actually who they said they were.

"That is perfectly all right. We only just got here, anyway," I said. "I, too, had a hard time finding where I was supposed to meet you."

The chauffeur smiled his appreciation and reached for my trunk, which Mr. Worthing handed over readily. As he loaded my luggage in the back of the car, Mrs. Worthing looped her arm through mine and walked with me to the curb.

"I am sorry for the circumstances under which we met, but I am glad we got to know one another, Rose," Mrs. Worthing said, placing her gloved hand on my forearm and squeezing.

"As am I," I said, squeezing her hand in return.

She beamed up at me and then pulled away as the chauffeur moved to open the passenger side door. But before he could, I saw a red smear on the silver handle. I recognized the rust color immediately.

Suddenly, I found myself beneath the familiarly warm sun of India, a cloud of dust enveloping me as I looked around, trying to understand why my ears were ringing, why my eyes burned. The people who had only moments before filled the street around our car, making the journey through Simla a slow one, had disappeared. The laughter and conversation I'd been ignoring in favor of my own thoughts had silenced. I turned my head, a simple movement that made me feel as though I were swimming through quicksand. Rose had been sitting beside me, but when I was finally able to focus on the spot where she'd been, I realized her seat was empty. My friend had disappeared to be replaced by a puddle of blood on the leather seat. The red liquid dripped from the upholstery onto the floor in thick rivulets. I leaned forward to make sense of it, not yet recognizing the horror before me. As I did, I noticed a hand in the backseat. Her hand. The long, delicate fingers of my friend, disconnected from her body.

I shook my head, trying to separate myself from the horror. I took deep breaths of the cool, London air and tried to focus on the movement around me. On the normalcy of everyday life continuing on despite my flashback.

"Are you feeling all right, Miss?"

The chauffeur's nerves had clearly been replaced by concern. His eyebrows were pulled together as he stooped down to peer into my face.

I blinked several times slowly. I wanted to respond, but everything felt far away, even my own thoughts. I turned to find the Worthings, but they were no longer behind me. They were halfway down the street, walking arm in arm.

"Miss?"

I looked back at the door handle, but the blood from

moments before was gone. The Chauffeur pulled the door open further and used a bare hand to direct me inside.

"Are you ready?" he asked.

My face reddened with embarrassment. "Yes, of course. I'm sorry."

I stepped into the car and let the chauffeur shut the door behind me. As he walked around the back of the car and hopped into the driver's seat, I took deep, calming breaths.

I couldn't allow myself to fall into my memories in that way. I needed to keep up appearances, which included not letting everyone around me think I was mad.

The blood had been in my imagination. Being back in a large city and climbing into a car had simply pushed my memories to the surface, jumbling them with the present. If there had been blood visible on the door, the Worthings would have seen it. The chauffeur would have seen it. Someone would have mentioned the oddity. But no one had, which meant I must have imagined it. That was the only logical explanation.

"All set, Miss?" the chauffeur asked over his shoulder as he put the car into gear.

The next time I got out of the car, I would be meeting Rose's relatives. My relatives. The people who could destroy the disguise I'd kept up this long. The people who could make everything I'd done up to this point useless. I took a deep breath, closed my eyes, and reminded myself of my ultimate goal. If I failed and the Beckinghams barred me from their home and Rose's inheritance, I wouldn't be the only person in dire straits.

My hand reached for the locket that was no longer around my neck, and when I found nothing there, my fingers instead brushed along my collar bone. I thought of the small scrap of paper I'd carried inside the locket for so long. Two words, scribbled in haste and faded with time: *help me.*

I leaned forward, placing my hand on the back of the front seat and smiled. "Yes, I'm ready."

I only hoped the words were true. I hoped I was ready. Then, I whispered to the young boy who had written that message. "Only a little longer now."

END OF EXCERPT

ABOUT THE AUTHOR

Blythe Baker is a thirty-something bottle redhead from the South Central part of the country. When she's not slinging words and creating new worlds and characters, she's acting as chauffeur to her children and head groomer to her household of beloved pets.

Blythe enjoys long walks with her dog on sweaty days, grubbing in her flower garden, cooking, and ruthlessly de-cluttering her overcrowded home. She also likes binge-watching mystery shows on TV and burying herself in books about murder.

To learn more about Blythe, visit her website and sign up for her newsletter at www.blythebaker.com

Made in the USA
San Bernardino, CA
17 August 2019